093

Berlie D

BBC

With special thanks to Mike James and Karen Johnson.

Published by BBC Educational Publishing, BBC White City, 201
Wood Lane, London W12 7TS
First published 2000
© Berlie Doherty/BBC Worldwide (Educational Publishing), 2000

The moral right of the author has been asserted.
Cover photograph © Andy Farrington, 2000

ISBN 0 563 54105 9

Printed and bound in Great Britain by Lawrence-Allen

Contents

Level one

Into the Crystal Caverns

A visitor in the night

Josie was in bed. And don't tell me she wasn't asleep, because she was. She was snoring. And in his house across the lane Peter was asleep too. So neither of them saw the blue-winged bug that came zizzing through the window and buzzing round the kitchen, first in Josie's house, then in Peter's. It did what it did so quickly and quietly that nobody saw it, and nobody heard, and if they had they would never have believed that a small blue-winged bug would have been clever enough to do such a thing. Then it flew out down the street to their school, trailing blue stars behind it.

The teacher, Miss Wordsworth, was sitting in front of the school computer. It was nine o'clock at night. She had come into school with some pieces of wood and cardboard that she was going to use with the children to create a Viking longboat. She had got quite carried away and started to build it, and then had got side-tracked into trying to make a Viking helmet so that she could wear it when she was telling them the story of Thor. Later, she took down the pictures of Scheherazade, Beowulf and the Snow Queen. They had always hung in the classroom, but she needed the space for Viking shields. She stowed the

paintings carefully in the stock cupboo
about to leave for home at last when she c.
the computer behind the bookshelves.

'Simon's game!' she chuckled. 'Oh, I must just ha₊
go at that before I leave.'

She told herself that it would be useful if she could
play it because she would be able to help Peter when he
had his turn tomorrow, but really she was dying to have
a go at it herself. Simon used to be one of her pupils, a
long time ago, and now he was grown up and
determined to be a computer wizard. His game, *Word
Master*, was going to bring him fame and fortune, he
was quite sure of that, but he had to make sure it
worked, so last week he brought it down to school and
asked the children to try it out for him.

'And you must be absolutely honest and tell me
what you think of it,' he had said, and then added,
because he just couldn't help it, 'It's brilliant!'

Everyone in the class who had tried it so far had
loved it, but no one had managed to reach the last level
and meet the Word Master himself, not even Francis,
the brightest boy in the class. He nearly got there, but
he failed to cross through the monster's lair before his
time ran out.

Miss Wordsworth looked at the class register where
the children who had already tried the game had
written their comments:

Matthew and Claire: It's brilliant!
Richard and Wendy: Best game ever!

Francis: It's like walking round your dreams. Can't wait to meet the Word Master!

Josie and Peter: Can't wait for our turn!

Miss Wordsworth smiled. She had never known the children to work so well at anything. She thought of Peter struggling to keep up with the others and hoped Josie wouldn't be too impatient with him.

'I'll just give myself half an hour,' she said, glancing at the clock. 'It shouldn't take me long to get the hang of it.' She switched on and pressed a few keys. 'Erm, not quite!' she thought, as strange flashes appeared on the screen. 'How come the children are always better at these things than I am? Ah, music – that sounds right. Here we go!'

The words YOU ARE NOW ENTERING THE WORLD OF THE WORD MASTER uncurled like wisps of smoke across the screen. Just as Miss Wordsworth touched the key that would take her into the Crystal Caverns and the first level of the game, she heard a slight buzzing coming from the classroom. She looked round the bookshelves and immediately saw the letters OTVURCVISIR on the whiteboard. One of the children must have been scribbling on it that afternoon. But surely she'd wiped it clean earlier?

'Never mind. Back to the game!'

But now the game looked different. The enticing, gleaming passages of the Crystal Caverns had gone dark, and instead there were yellow words on the screen: RUN VIRUS. YES OR NO?

'Oh dear,' Miss Wordsworth sighed. 'Now what? I could do with a bit of help with this!'

The Help icon on the corner of the screen lit up and a smiling face appeared, flashing sparkling white teeth.

'Do you need help?' he asked, as polite and charming as a dentist.

'Yes!' Miss Wordsworth typed, relieved.

The Help icon beamed at her, and now she could see a yellow glow round his head, filling the screen like the rising sun. He really did have a very charming smile.

'I mean no!' she gasped, suddenly worried. 'No!' she typed.

'Too late to change your mind!' The charming Help icon flashed his smile at her. 'But congratulations. You have made the right choice.'

Relieved, Miss Wordsworth switched off the computer. 'That was a close thing,' she said to herself. 'And in future, I'll leave it to the children!' She stood up and noticed again the writing on the board. OTVURCVISIR. She stared at it for a moment, puzzled, and then wiped it clean.

The owls are watching in the trees and the cats are prowling homewards. The moonlight is ghostly and silver. It slides through the window of Josie's kitchen and lights up the fridge. A heap of magnetic letters are stuck together on the lino tiles, and the ones that are left on the door make no sense at all. OTVURCVISIR.

otVurcVisir

The next morning, as soon as she woke up, Josie remembered that she was going to be playing the *Word Master* game. Brilliant! What she hoped more than anything was that she was going to be able to beat Francis and meet the Word Master himself. The only trouble was that she was going to be playing it with Peter. He was the youngest boy in the class and he was miles behind her in everything. She knew he would drag her back and be a nuisance. She would much rather be playing the game with Ellie. Josie helped herself to cereal and ate it slowly, daydreaming that Peter was late for school and that she romped through the levels all on her own.

Her mother hurried into the kitchen with Josie's baby brother under one arm and a pile of washing under the other. The first thing she saw was a heap of magnetic letters on the floor under the fridge.

'Josie, did you make this mess?'

Josie's mouth was full of cornflakes. 'Mmm. Mmm.' She shook her head.

'Well, somebody did. You sort them out, please.'

Josie went to the fridge and stared at the letters that were still on the door. OTVURCVISIR. She started to move them about to make words: SIR, TOUR, VIV . . .

'Never mind that,' said Mum. 'Breakfast.'

Josie went back to the table, staring thoughtfully at the letters.

In the red house across the street, Peter was eating scrambled eggs. Peter's mother opened up her fridge to get ice-cubes for the orange juice. She nearly dropped the tray. Every cube had a letter of the alphabet inside it, like scrabble squares.

'Is this your doing, Peter?' she asked.

Peter came and looked. 'No,' he said. 'It doesn't even say anything. OTVURCVISIR.' He shook the ice-cubes onto the kitchen table and slid them round. 'Cut,' he wrote.

'Hmm.' His mother leaned over his shoulder. 'Visit,' she suggested. 'Or visitor, that's a good one.'

Immediately, the ice-cubes slid about and started to make two words. At the very same moment, the magnetic letters on Josie's fridge started to slide about too. And they made the same two words.

Simon was still in bed. 'Victor Virus,' he muttered in his sleep, tossing this way and that. 'Victor Virus. Go away! Go away!' He sat up in bed, his eyes wide with horror, staring at his own white face in the mirror opposite. 'Victor Virus! Why do you keep haunting me? I don't want you in my game. I've got rid of you once. Leave my game alone!' Then he realised that he had been having a nightmare. He lay back on his pillow and switched out the light. 'It's all right,' he told himself. 'Stop worrying. You binned Victor Virus, remember. He's gone for good.' And he went back to sleep.

To Josie's annoyance, Peter wasn't late for school. He and Francis came running up the street behind her and Ellie.

'It's our turn to go on the game today,' he shouted, leaping past her like a noisy puppy.

'And you'd better not do anything stupid,' she said.

Peter ignored her. He was too excited to mind anyway.

'It's brilliant!' Francis said. 'It mixes your brains up and makes them go fizzy.'

'He hasn't got any brains,' said Josie. She and Ellie giggled.

'Wish I didn't have to play it with her. I know she'll get all the answers and I won't get any,' Peter muttered to Francis.

'She is pretty brainy. Bet she won't meet the Word Master, though.'

'Did you?'

Francis screwed up his face as if he couldn't quite

remember. 'Well – nearly! If Miss Wordsworth hadn't stopped me I'd have got there. Easily.'

'Wow!'

Peter threw an imaginary ball high up into the trees by the school. He couldn't wait, even though he did have to play it with Josie.

Miss Wordsworth was standing in the middle of a half-finished longboat. She was dressed as a Viking.

'Good morning, everybody,' she called as they filed in. 'We're going to have an adventure today! You're all going to help me finish this longboat and we're going to sail away in it!'

'You look funny, Miss Wordsworth,' said Ellie.

'Do I?' asked Miss Wordsworth, stroking her chin thoughtfully. 'Perhaps I need a beard to make me look fiercer. Anyone fancy making me one?'

They all shot up their hands.

'Wonderful! But not Peter and Josie.' Miss Wordsworth smiled at them. 'They're going to be having adventures of their own.'

Josie stood up, blushing slightly. This was going to be the best day of her life. She was going to beat Francis to the Word Master! As long as Peter didn't mess about, she was sure she could do it.

'Good luck!' Ellie whispered. 'Go for it!'

'Don't look so worried, Peter,' said Miss Wordsworth. 'If you get stuck, click on the Help icon. He's very useful.'

'Have you played it, Miss?' Francis asked.

Miss Wordsworth nodded, smiling.

'Did you meet the Word Master?'

'Ah, that would be telling!' she laughed. 'Off you go, you two. Enjoy it!'

'Can I set it up for them?' Francis asked.

Miss Wordsworth nodded. 'But be quick. I need you too.'

As soon as Josie and Peter had reached the bookshelves, they raced to the computer. They both wanted to be the first to use the joystick. They wrestled with it, nearly knocking Francis out of the chair.

'Me first,' said Peter. 'I was here first.' He put his break-time biscuit down on the seat by way of claiming it.

'Only because you ran. I should go first.'

'Stop messing about,' Francis said. 'There's two joysticks anyway.' He switched on the machine. The words YOU ARE NOW ENTERING THE WORLD OF THE WORD MASTER came up. Peter and Josie giggled with excitement. 'You have to work your way through the Crystal Caverns first. That's the easy part.'

'We can manage on our own now,' Josie said, pulling the joystick away from Peter again.

'OK. Good luck, Peter,' and Francis turned his back on them, which was a shame because he just missed seeing a most amazing thing. Tiny flashes of electric sparks lit up the air around the computer screen like a firework show; greens and reds, and dazzling blues and whites, and then a yellow glow that was as sharp as lemons.

'Ready,' he heard Josie say.

'Steady!' Peter laughed.

'Go!' they both shouted at once. Francis turned round quickly. There was a rushing sound like a great wind among the trees, and Josie and Peter felt themselves being lifted up and up, and whirled round and round, spinning and whizzing, faster, and smaller, and brighter, and then – they disappeared.

The lost children

Simon rolled out of bed when the alarm went off. He nearly squashed the cat, which hissed and spat and dived down the stairs to safety, leaping out of the cat-flap. He crawled to the bathroom and splashed himself awake, and then he remembered his big task of the day. He needed to write a new anti-virus program for his game. He ran back into the bedroom and switched on his computer. All around him were his cardboard models of castles and mines and strange-looking creatures with twisted faces and eyes that glowed in the dark, knights in shining armour and skeletons with dangly arms and hungry grins. They were all 3-D designs for his game, and they'd taken months to make.

He sat down at his keyboard, but all he could think about was whether the children liked his game or not.

'They'll love it, bound to. They'll be mobbing me for my autograph! I'll be famous! I'll be on the front of T-shirts!'

He tossed a fluffy model of a green man up in the air and stuffed it head first into an empty coffee cup.

'But what if they don't like it? What if they can't make it work, or it's too simple? What if it's too hard? I shouldn't have binned that Help program. Nah, they don't need help. They're clever! What if they're too clever? What if they laugh at it?'

He sat with his head in his hands. The green man keeled over sideways.

'It's no good. I'll just have to go and find out. Now!'

He picked up his rucksack, jammed a notebook and pencils into it and ran out of the bedroom. A second later, he ran back in and picked up the green man.

'I can't do this on my own, Green Man. Come and give me some moral support.' He stuffed it in his rucksack and ran out again.

Simon lived about two miles away from the school. When he was younger he had been a pupil there, so he knew exactly how long it would take him to get there on his bike, but the nearer he got to school, the more nervous he felt. What if they hated it?

When he arrived in the classroom, hot and breathless, he was still wearing his yellow cycling helmet. He nearly fell over the half-built Viking ship that was propped across the doorway.

'It's Simon!' the children called out. Most of them were kneeling on the floor measuring pieces of cardboard and cutting up strips of cloth. Miss Wordsworth was helping Oliver to draw a shield.

'It's the biking Viking!' she laughed, looking up at Simon. 'We're being invaded, children!'

'Morning, Miss Wordsworth. Hi, everyone.' Simon took a deep breath and blurted it out. 'Well, what d'you think of the game? It's OK, you can tell me the truth. I can take it. On the chin!' He sat down on Katie's pencil-case. The children looked at him in silence. He gulped noisily. 'Mmm. OK. It's bad.'

'Stop teasing him,' Miss Wordsworth said.

All the children spoke at once, clamouring for Simon's attention.

'It's brilliant!'

'Best game ever!'

'Excellent!'

'They all love it,' Miss Wordsworth told him.

Simon let out his breath at last, making a rubbery sound through his lips. 'Great. You had me worried for a minute. I just want to write a new program for it.' He headed for the computer area, stepping over bits of armour.

'Josie and Peter have just started their turn. Oh, and turf Francis out, will you?' Miss Wordsworth called. 'He's had his go. He'd stay on it all day if I let him. Now, everyone, I need carpenters, measurers and designers . . .'

Simon climbed over the piles of cardboard and went round the back of the bookshelves. He was surprised to find Francis there on his own, frantically working the controls. The screen was blank.

'Hi,' Simon said.

Francis didn't even look up. But then Francis was like that when he was absorbed in something; he just went as deaf as a post.

'I thought you'd had your go. Where's Josie and Peter?'

Francis looked up at last. His face was ashen.

'They've just – I don't know – Simon – they just – there were all these sparks and lights and – they're in it!' His words bubbled out, making no sense at all.

Simon laughed. 'Try again.'

'They're in the game!'

'Yeah, and I've got two heads.'

'Look for yourself!'

The Dream Cave

It was as dark as midnight. Josie was lying on the ground. All she could hear was a steady drip, drip, drip, all around her. Drip. Drip. She stretched out her fingers and felt the ground underneath her. It was cold and damp, chilly as river water. Drip drip. Drip drip. She sat up slowly, feeling around her. She tried to stand up and found she was in a tight, cramped space that closed down over her head.

'Where am I?' she said out loud, and back came her own voice, tiny and scared, *'Where am I? Am I? Am I?'*

Peter was lying with his eyes wide open, trying to make sense of the cold blackness around him and the icy splash of water on his face. When he heard Josie's voice he stood up quickly and banged his head on the roof.

'Ouch!' he shouted, and his echo answered him. *'Ouch! Ch! Ch!'*

'Peter! Is that you?' Josie called. 'Where are you?' *'Are you? Are you?'*

He crouched down, rubbing his sore head. 'I don't know, Josie,' he shouted back. 'Where are you?' *'You? You?'*

Back in the classroom, Simon and Francis peered into the screen. The picture on it was very dim, with just a swirl of black shapes.

'There! Did you hear Peter's voice?' Francis said.

The voices came again, far away and faint and frightened, and echoing round and round.

'Peter, is that you? Where are you?'

'I don't know, Josie.'

Simon stared at the machine in disbelief. 'What's going on?' he asked. 'What are you three playing at?'

'You heard them,' Francis said. 'They're in the game!' He stared at Simon, and his eyes were so wide with worry and fright that Simon knew he wasn't making things up. Whatever it was that was going on, Francis was as puzzled about it as he was.

'I don't believe it. I just don't believe it,' Simon said again.

'Neither do I.'

They could hear the tiny voices again, calling to each other. Could Josie and Peter have set up some kind of recording? But the voices were definitely coming from the computer's own little speaker. It just didn't make sense.

'Shall I tell Miss Wordsworth?' Francis asked.

'No, wait a bit. There must be an explanation. They can't – they can't really be in it!' Simon tried to laugh. The idea was ridiculous! And yet he could definitely hear their voices.

'D'you think there could be a virus?' asked Francis.

Simon shook his head. 'I don't see how there can be. Don't touch anything. Just keep an eye on it.'

He went round the bookshelves into the main class area. Miss Wordsworth had her back to him, kneeling between Oliver and Ellen. Oliver was drawing a pattern on a shield, carefully, his tongue sticking out between his teeth.

'Miss Wordsworth,' Simon said.

She turned round, smiling brightly, an orange tissue-paper beard dangling from her chin. 'Everything OK in there?'

'Er – fine,' said Simon. It was impossible to tell her the truth. He just couldn't find the right words. 'I just wondered – did anyone else touch the game this morning?'

'This morning? No? Is there a problem?'

'Oh no – no problem. Josie and Peter are having a bit of trouble. Er – I'll keep an eye on them for you.'

Miss Wordsworth put her hand to her mouth. Could she have done something when she played it last night? There was that strange message . . . but Simon had gone behind the screen, and as soon as she stood up to follow him, Ellie came crying to her with a Viking helmet pulled right down over her head.

'It's stuck, Miss Wordsworth!'

It took a good five minutes to get it off, and lots of cuddles to make Ellie better afterwards.

'Simon, quick!' Francis called. Simon hurried back to the computer area.

22

'What's happened?'

'I've just seen a blue thing flashing across the screen.'

'A blue thing?'

'I've never seen that before. D'you think it's a bug?'

Simon shook his head. 'No, can't be.' He looked at Francis hopelessly. He couldn't be sure of anything any more.

Francis shrugged. 'What is it then?'

Down the dark corridors of the Crystal Caverns, a little blue bug with shiny wings was flying, intent on his mission. His antennae picked up the voices of Josie and Peter calling to each other and he paused, listening carefully. Was this the enemy he had come to destroy? He drew closer. It seemed to be some kind of invasion, and yet there were only two of them. And they reminded him of the human people who peered into the Cyberworld from the other side. Little human people in some kind of distress. How did they get in? And should he help them or destroy them?

'Zip zap zee, how can I do my job if there's humans all over the place? How did they get in here? Here I am, super-virus-buster Zzaap, hot on the trail of Victor Virus – and I find that two humans have invaded the game as well! It's so hard being a super-hero! As if I hadn't got enough to do! What now?' He zigzagged down the passage, buzzing to himself. 'I suppose the best thing is to get them out of this level as fast as I can and send them off to the Word Master. He'll deal with them.'

Josie was afraid to move backwards or forwards in the dark. She crouched in the tunnel as if she had been turned to stone. Then she heard a zizzy voice, a bit like a bee humming.

'OK. Come on, this way. Come on, this way, this way, crouch and touch, crouch and touch.'

A blue light like a dragon-fly was humming round her, darting so swiftly that she couldn't make out what it was. At first she thought it was somebody waving a tiny torch. And now she could see that she was in a long, low tunnel with glistening, mossy walls. Water dripped like slow raindrops, splish, splish, splish, and trickled over the rocky pathway under her feet.

The blue light danced away from her. 'Come on, come on. Crouch and touch, crouch and touch,' came the buzzy voice again.

She followed very cautiously. Now she could see that the tunnel opened up into a huge cavern, and as soon as she saw that, and knew her way forward, the blue light disappeared. She was in darkness again.

'Crouch and touch,' she repeated to herself. She began to move slowly forward. 'Crouch and touch.'

Peter was still nursing his sore head. Suddenly, his tunnel was flooded with blue light. He stood up and banged his head again. 'Ouch!'

'Crouch, not ouch!' a buzzy voice said. The blue light flickered away, and the voice hummed cheerfully. 'Crouch, not ouch!'

Peter bent down and began to grope forward, holding out one hand in front of him and the other over his head, just in case. And next time he looked up, he saw that he was in a deep, high chamber, and that Josie was standing in the middle of it. The blue light had gone.

The chamber was softly lit by green eyes hanging in lanterns from the walls. Josie was holding one of them up

high above her head, and gazing round at the most beautiful sight in the world.

'They're in the Dream Cave!' breathed Francis, staring at the screen. 'Oh, the lucky lollipops! Fancy actually being there!'

'Never mind that!' groaned Simon. 'How on earth are they going to get out of it?'

'Shall I tell Miss Wordsworth?'

'No!' said Simon. 'Not yet. You try and keep her away from here. I'm going to try and programme them out.'

The ceiling of the Dream Cave was spiked with rock-like icicles, gleaming wet and golden, some twisted round like the horns of unicorns, some almost touching other spikes that rose out of the ground to meet them, like reaching fingers.

'Oh, magic!' breathed Peter.

'They're stalactites,' said Josie. 'Stalactites hold tight. That's how I remember them. And the ones that stick up from the ground are stalagmites.'

Peter reached out to touch one.

'Careful!' Josie said. 'They're thousands of years old!'

And just as she said that, he touched the stalactite. It chimed softly, glowing.

'Hey, get that! It sounds like a bell.'

'Peter. Stop messing. Have you any idea where we are?'

The eye inside Josie's lantern began to close, and as it did so, the light began to fade. All the eyes in the other lanterns closed. All they had was the single light of the glowing stalactite. Strange creases and lines began to appear in the rock wall, bumps like noses, juts like chins, sticky-out bits like ears, cracks like mouths.

'We're in a cave of some sort,' Peter replied.

'I know that. But how did we get here? We were in the classroom a few minutes ago.'

They stared at each other. Could they both be dreaming? Josie tried to force herself to remember what had happened.

'We were about to play Simon's game –'

'And you grabbed my joystick –'

'No, you grabbed my joystick –'

'There were flashes and sparks –'

'And now we're –'

'In the game. This is it! This is just what Francis wrote: like walking round your dreams.'

'But what if we can't get out of it?' Josie said. 'What if we're stuck here?'

They both went very quiet. And from far down one of the long tunnels came the deep sinister sound of laughter.

Zzaap left the children and followed the sound of laughter. He flew down a long, dark tunnel that dripped and oozed green slime and stank of foul water. At last, he came to something that was like a black hole in space. It was hung with waving ribbons that had computer images of Josie and Peter on them. Zzaap saw a pair of gleaming eyes, and a figure dressed in black. He switched off his blue light and approached silently. He had located the enemy of the game, and in all his time of tracking down enemies he had never come across anything so sinister. He could hear him speaking softly to himself.

'Trapped! Trapped! Trapped for ever, my dear humans! Victor Virus has you in his power.'

Rock Face

'Well zip zap zee! Here's a puzzle,' Zzaap mused. 'I've located the enemy virus. I could zap him now. But what about these humans? What will happen to them if I zap him?'

He moved in a bit closer. Victor Virus was chattering to himself in a high-pitched whine.

'How dare Simon try to wipe me out of his game! Now let him suffer! Miss Wordsworth has activated my power. She has only to speak to me again and I will be strong enough to meet the Word Master himself! I'll leave this game and take these humans with me. They will give me the brainpower I need to rule Cyberspace!'

As he was talking, he twisted a yellow pen in his long, spindly fingers, making it glow. Zzaap backed away from it, sensing its power even at a distance.

'Hmm,' thought Zzaap. 'So that's what he wants. This is going to be a foxy problem, even for a super-hero like me. And meanwhile the humans seem to have no idea how to move on. This is a tricky game, this is. Trust me to get stuck in a word game, and I can't even read!'

He left Victor Virus rubbing his smooth hands

together and headed back to where Josie and Peter were sitting slumped in thought by the single light of a stalactite.

'It's so dark here,' Josie said. She touched a stalagmite, and it glowed like the stalactite, chiming softly.

'Gently,' she said. 'Don't break it,' as Peter reached out to touch another one. Soon they were both jumping up and down, laughing, and the cave was pealing like a country church.

'They're having a lot of fun,' said Francis enviously, as Miss Wordsworth called him back into the classroom. He looked back over his shoulder, trying to hear what was going on behind the bookshelves.

'Is everything all right in there? Francis? Hello, Francis?'

'Oh – fine.'

'That's lovely. It's nice to know that they're working so well together. And it means they can manage without your help – but I can't!'

Miss Wordsworth had a way of making everyone feel special. Usually, Francis would have done anything in the world for her, but today there was only one place where he wanted to be. As soon as Miss Wordsworth turned her back, he sidled round the bookshelves again.

Peter was staring at the strange knobbles and cracks and creases in the cave wall. 'Ever heard of a rock face?'

And as soon as he said it, the rock face opened its eyes, which were as green as moss, and wiggled its ears, and arched its eyebrows, and opened its mouth and yawned, showing a row of spiky brown teeth.

'At long last!' it rumbled in a gravelly voice. 'I have maintained a stony silence for long enough, but I grow bolder by the minute. Get it! Hah, laugh then!'

As it laughed, little pebbles rolled out of its mouth.

'Can you help us?' Peter said bravely. After all, nothing seemed strange any more. Why shouldn't rocks talk? 'We're trying to get out and . . .' he gazed round him. Three tunnels led away from the Dream Cave. 'We can't remember which tunnel we came down. They all look the same.'

'Hmm.' The rock face creased into frowns. 'A gritty problem. You could wander round for years in these tunnels and never see the light of day again. But it's no good going back the way you came. There's going to be a rock fall there. I can feel it in my seams. And –' tears trickled down its cheeks, 'lots of little stones will be buried alive. It's a terrible thing. And if you get caught in it your bones will be crushed to sand. If you want to get out of here you'll have to speak to the Word Master. No short cuts!' The rock face sighed. Its great eyelids drooped. Only slits of mossy lights showed. 'I need another thousand year's sleep. No talk left.'

'But which way?' Peter asked.

But the eye glints had disappeared, and the ears were just knobbles in the rock. Only the mouth was left.

'Collect the pebbles,' it muttered. The mouth closed up into a tight little crack.

Peter scooped up the pile of pebbles and put some of them in his rucksack. He left the rest at the mouth of one of the tunnels, then started to run down it, into the darkness that was like a great yawn. He stopped so suddenly that Josie charged into him, nearly dropping her eye-lantern. 'Listen! Rocks are falling!'

From the throat of the tunnel came the long, heavy rumble of falling stones.

'Oh, the poor little stones,' Josie said. 'They'll be crushed to powder.'

'So will we if we carry on. Turn back.'

They ran back into the Dream Cave. A voice echoed down one of the other tunnels. 'This way, this way!'

One of Rock Face's eyes opened and closed again as they ran past him and down a second tunnel. Green slime oozed and dripped from the roof and the walls. The stones under their feet were as slippery as ice. A boom of deep laughter echoed around them. And in his lair, Victor Virus drew bats out of dark air, making them swoop and dive down the tunnel's wet, black throat.

'Where are they going?' Simon asked Francis. 'I didn't put that tunnel in the game.'

'It wasn't there when I played it. Can't you stop them?'

Zzaap switched his light back on. 'Zip zap zee,' he muttered to himself. 'Don't the humans have any brains? Don't go down there!' And he zipped after Josie and Peter.

'Hey! I've just seen the virus!' Francis shouted. 'There was a blue light – just then – didn't you see it? You should be running your anti-virus program.'

Simon's heart sank. If only he'd set it up before he brought the game to school. 'I can't.'

Francis stared at him. 'Why not?'

'Because there isn't one. Not any more.'

'What? First rule of computer programming: write an anti-virus program. Even I know that, and I'm only nine years old!'

Simon had taught Francis everything he knew about computer programming. It hurt him to have it all thrown back in his face like this, especially when he knew that Francis was right.

'I did write a program,' Simon explained. 'He was really good. He was linked to the Help program and his name was Victor Virus – the conqueror of viruses.'

'Brilliant. So what happened?'

'He wasn't working properly so I binned him. And – yes, I should have set another one up before I brought the game here. Didn't think I'd really need one.'

Francis shook his head. Some grown-ups really needed looking after. 'Well, we need one now.'

The tunnel was suddenly bathed in brilliant blue light. Josie covered up her eyes.

'I can't see where I'm going!'

'It's that buzzy thing again,' Peter said. 'It's blinding me.'

'We'll have to turn back.'

Snarls twitched round their feet like whips as they stumbled back into the Dream Cave again.

'I can't remember which tunnel we have to try next!' Josie panted. 'Oh, quickly, quickly, which way?'

'That one on the right is the one with the rock fall,' said Peter. 'I left the pebbles there so we'd know.'

Peter scooped up the pebbles and put them in his rucksack. A gravelly chuckle came from nowhere. Two mossy glints in the rock face opened, and then shut tight.

The Rhyme-Chime Chamber

One tunnel opened up into another, like the strands of a spider's web. Zzaap flew round their heads.

'Turn back!' he buzzed.

But they didn't understand and kept on running, flapping their hands round their heads to shoo him off.

'All right, ignore me!' He flew off in the opposite direction. Maybe they would come to their senses and follow him. But they were tired and frightened by now, and it was impossible to tell which passage was which any more.

Victor Virus smiled to himself as he watched them.

'All on your own, little humans? Getting tired? Have a rest. There's a convenient cave just in front of you.' He flicked his power pen, and immediately a cave lit up out of the darkness.

Josie and Peter stumbled into it. They were in a huge chamber made of massive slanting slabs of rock, shining golden and green like leaves and grass in sunshine.

'It's like a hall,' said Josie. 'A place for a ball.'

Peter stared at her. There was something strange about the way she was talking. He shivered. 'It's cold in here. Let's get out.'

But as he turned, there came a rumble of falling rocks across the entrance to the chamber. A boulder the size of a house rolled across the entrance.

'No!' Josie shouted. She hammered on the wall of fallen rock. 'We're trapped! Help! Help!'

'Don't shout,' said Peter. 'They'll never hear us through these stones.'

'We'll die in here.'

'Two heaps of bones.'

Josie turned on Peter angrily. 'Why are you making fun of me? It's serious Peter, can't you see?' She put her hands to her mouth as if she were trying to stop the words coming out. 'I did it then! I talked in rhyme!'

'You seem to be doing it all the time,' said Peter scornfully, then he realised what he'd said. 'Hey! I did it too! We're going mad!'

Simon groaned. 'You know where they are, don't you?'

'The Rhyme-Chime Chamber,' Francis giggled. 'Don't they sound silly. It's like watching a pantomime.'

At that moment, Miss Wordsworth put her head round the bookshelves. 'Break-time!'

Simon and Francis both jumped.

'Come on, you two!' Miss Wordsworth laughed. 'I see Josie and Peter have gone out already!'

Francis stood up quickly with his back to the computer screen. 'They've been working really hard.'

'And you need a break too. Come on!' Laughing, Miss Wordsworth reached behind him and switched off the computer.

Simon and Francis stared at each other, horrified.

'But we haven't saved the game!' Francis whispered.

'We've lost them,' Simon whispered. 'We'll never get them back now.'

Miss Wordsworth turned round. 'What are you talking about? They'll come in straight after break. Go on you two – a spot of fresh air will do you both good.'

She steered them round the longboat and out of the classroom, and then headed off to the staff room. Francis and Simon stared after her in despair.

'They were nearly out of that level!' Francis groaned. 'They'll have to start all over again.'

'If they're still alive. They haven't even been saved in the computer memory. They might just be computer sprites for the rest of their lives.'

Victor Virus strolled smoothly down the passageways that led to the Rhyme-Chime Chamber. Zzaap sensed his movements immediately.

'Get the humans out of Victor Virus's way first,' he told himself. 'You've had some sticky problems, super-intellect Zzaap, but nothing as sticky as this.' He could hear Josie and Simon shouting through the rock wall. 'They're sounding strangely poetical! Must be something alphabetical!' And he squeezed through a crack the size of a grain of sand. 'Cheer up,' he buzzed, switching on his light.

'We're going mad!' Peter was saying.

'Don't look so sad,' Zzaap buzzed. 'Hey! That wasn't bad! A rhyming Zzaap! I didn't know I was such a clever so-and-so.'

Peter groaned.

'Please help us,' Josie sobbed. 'We're in a trap.'

'Yes, I can see that too.' Zzaap zipped from one corner of the chamber to the other, looking for holes or exits of any kind that the children might squeeze through. There was nothing. 'Well, it seems that you must spend your lives here, speaking verse.'

'I can't think of anything worse,' moaned Peter. 'Stop buzzing, insect!'

'Insect! I'm Zzaap, the sensational intellect!'

'Then help us, please. You only came to mock and tease. Oh, I didn't mean it really. Everything I say sounds silly!' Peter sat down on the cold floor and crossed his arms in despair. It was better not to talk at all if this was the best he could do.

Zzaap buzzed round him and Josie, full of sympathy. He hummed a nice little tune to try to cheer them up but it didn't help much.

'You will escape. There'll be a time
When you speak a word that doesn't rhyme.
It really won't take much detection
You'll find it in your own reflection.'

And with that, he disappeared.

Josie and Peter looked at each other helplessly. Josie sighed.

'What reflection? The only thing that I can see is you, Peter!'

'And lots of things rhyme with Peter. Litre, metre, heater. How about Josie! Nosy. Dozy.'

Josie stamped round the chamber, frustrated. 'No,

that's not it.' Suddenly, she saw a large mirror on the wall of the chamber. It definitely wasn't there before. She stopped. 'I've got it! Mirror! Tell me a word that rhymes with mirror!'

They looked at each other, searching for words. They put out their hands disbelievingly to touch their reflections, and walked right through.

Nervously, Simon switched on the computer. 'Come on, come on! Why does it have to be so slow?'

The caverns came up. He scanned all the tunnels and chambers. The Dream Cave, the Rhyme-Chime Chamber. Empty, every one of them.

'We're too late,' he groaned. 'They've gone.'

Level two

HET STECLA
FO GOLOM

The Wall of Spikes

As Josie and Peter walked through the mirror they heard strange sounds – the clattering of bones, moaning voices, the clanking of chains, and the sweet sound of a woman's voice singing. When they emerged, they found themselves in a room with tiny slit windows.

'Well, we're not in the Crystal Caverns any more,' said Peter. 'But it's not much warmer, is it.'

'I wonder if we're on the next level? I bet we are! We're in a castle! Look at the spiral staircase. They make me dizzy, these.' Josie ran to the twisting stairs and started to go up them.

'Careful!' Peter warned. 'You don't know where they might lead to.'

'Are you scared or something?' Josie said over her shoulder. 'We can't just sit and wait for something to happen you know.'

Peter ran after her. The steps were steep and winding, getting narrower and narrower, and then, at a small landing, they divided and disappeared up into the dark and cobwebby shadows.

'You go that way, and I'll go this way,' Peter suggested.

'No,' said Josie, 'whatever happens we must stick together.'

'Now who's scared?'

'If there's puzzles to solve we can do them better together.'

'Can we?' Peter was secretly pleased. It seemed to him that Josie had done most of the thinking up till now. 'Two heads are better than one!'

He pointed up to two heads carved in stone that were gazing down at them.

'Never mind them. We'll have to choose which way to go. Left or right?' asked Josie.

The heads both opened their mouths at the same time.

'Left!' one shouted.

'Right!' shouted the other.

'I've found them!' Simon shouted. 'They're on the next level.'

He and Francis peered at the screen and saw the two small figures climbing up the spiral stairs.

'Lucky lollipops,' said Francis. 'They're in the Castle of Gloom. I love this one. It's really creepy. D'you think they're going to manage? I mean, even this first bit is hard. If they go the wrong way they'll get stuck on the Wall of Spikes.'

'I know, I know,' said Simon. 'Look, hadn't you better go out? It's supposed to be playtime. Now we know Josie and Peter are still in the game, I'm going to get on with writing an anti-virus program.'

More than anything, Francis wanted to stay and watch, maybe even help. But he knew Simon was right. Miss Wordsworth was probably standing at the staff room window at that very moment, looking out to make sure he was in the playground. She might be looking for Josie and Peter as well. He saw Peter's chocolate biscuit and bit it in half.

'Pity to waste it.'

Gloomily, Simon watched him go. He had no idea whether anything he did was going to make any difference. How on earth had a virus got into the game anyway? He'd have to worry about that later. He started typing numbers into his computer. Then he stopped and shook his head.

'It's weird, though. So many things going wrong! It feels as if it's not my game any more.'

He started typing again, stretched, walked round the classroom, deep in thought, and saw Peter's biscuit. Without even knowing what he was doing, he finished it off and sat down at the computer again.

'I'm starving,' grumbled Peter. 'There must be something to eat in this place. Perhaps one of these stairways leads to food. Left or right?'

'Left!' shouted one stone head.

'Go right!' yelled the other.

'Honestly, Peter, you're a pig,' Josie said. 'How can you think of food at a time like this?'

And then they heard a sound like teeth clacking together, and a wavery voice calling, 'Food? Did someone mention food?'

'Left!' Josie decided. They turned left in the direction of the voice and went up the staircase, which led straight into a room that was flickering with shadows in the pale light of a yellow, waxy candle. All the walls were covered in spikes, and from nearly every spike, skulls and skeletons were hanging, hooked by their bony armpits or their eye sockets.

'Anybody there?' came a chorus of croaking voices. 'Anybody to spare?'

'Nobody's having my body!' Peter shouted bravely. One of the skeletons waved his rattling hand.

'Welcome, Josie and Peter. Skinless is my name. Come and hang from your spikes. They're very comfortable, after a hundred years or so.' His teeth rattled loosely in his jaw as he laughed.

'We're looking for food, that's all,' said Josie. She could feel her own bones rattling with fright.

'Food!' the skeleton sighed. 'Haven't eaten for ages. That's how I got to be the way I am now. Oh yes, you've come the right way, if it's food you're talking about. But if you're not talking about food, you'd better find your spike.'

He waved his hand, and they could see their names – *Josie* over one of the spikes, *Peter* over another.

'Chant me some food and I'll spare you the spikes. Oh, chant me some food to cheer up my cheekbones, there's good chaps, to dribble down my chinny chin, to chew and to chomp, to munch and to crunch! Hmm? Can you do that, children?'

'It's another puzzle,' Josie whispered to Peter. 'I bet he wants some 'c-h' words. Like – cheese.' Immediately, a hunk of yellow cheese appeared in front of them.

'Mmm, smell that pong!' Skinless chortled. 'Reminds me of the days when I used to have feet!'

Peter broke off a piece and handed it to him. The skeleton shook his head.

'Somebody will have to eat it for me, I'm afraid. It might choke me.'

'I will!' Peter bit into the cheese. It was very tasty – the tangy sort that makes your eyes water. Josie hated it.

'Choose something else!' Skinless begged. 'You've set my stomach memory rumbling now.'

'Chops,' said Josie, and they appeared on a wooden plate, swimming in rich, oniony, steaming gravy.

Skinless sniffed and grinned, but waved his bony fingers when Josie offered him the plate.

'You have them. Bring me something else, quick.'

'Chips!' Peter suggested. Nothing happened.

'Never heard of them,' Skinless said.

'Chocolate?'

Again nothing happened.

'Chips and chocolate?' Skinless shook his head. 'These must be modern inventions.'

'Chilli. Chapattis,' suggested Josie. Skinless stared at her in puzzled silence.

'Chicken!' Peter shouted. A roast chicken floated in front of them. Skinless rubbed his fingerbones with glee.

'My favourite thing! Eat up!'

'I don't eat meat,' Peter moaned.

'I'll have it,' said Josie. She was so full that she could hardly walk to the plate. 'You'll have to think of something else – like chestnuts!'

A plate of roasted chestnuts appeared. They smelt delicious. Skinless stabbed one on the end of his finger and sniffed it happily. Peter put some of them in his rucksack for later.

'I think we'd better get out of here,' Josie said when all the plates were empty, 'before I burst. Skinless is happy anyway.'

Skinless was fast asleep, snoring peacefully, but as Peter and Josie stood up to leave, he stretched out his bony arms and wrapped them round them.

'Just a little something sweet to finish up,' he pleaded. 'I always was partial to a bit of pudding.'

'Cherry pie!' Peter laughed.

'Perfect.'

A long time later, feeling very full and much more cheerful, Peter and Josie turned to leave the Wall of Spikes. But their way was barred by a rusty knight.

Victor Virus had just found the mirror on the wall when he felt a pain where his heart might have been, if he had one.

'What's happening?' he panted. 'Who's doing that to me?'

Simon finished typing and leaned back in his chair, exhausted. 'There! That should sort it!'

He decided to walk round the yard a bit to clear his head. Francis was playing goalie between two sweatshirts. When he saw Simon in the yard he ran up to him, to shouts of rage from Matthew and jubilation from Tom, who had just kicked the ball through.

'What's up with you today?' Matthew yelled. 'You're useless!'

Francis didn't even hear him. 'Any luck?' he asked Simon.

'I think so. But I still can't understand how a virus could have got in there.'

They both shook their heads.

'It's a mystery,' Francis agreed, 'but it doesn't matter now, as long as it's zapped.'

'I suppose so. Anyway, I desperately need a cup of coffee and a choccie biccie. I'll see if I can raid the staff room.' Simon walked away, deep in thought. Then he stopped. Hadn't he just eaten a chocolate biscuit? He could still taste it. But where had it come from? He shook his head again. Another mystery.

Miss Wordsworth was watching them both from the staff room window. She could see that they both looked very worried. Could there be something wrong with the game, she wondered. Poor Simon. It meant so much to him. And then she remembered again the few moments she had spent on the computer the night before. Had she done anything that could be causing problems? Wouldn't it be a good idea just to have a look now, while the classroom was empty? It would be wonderful if she could put it right again. Then Simon would stop worrying and Francis would help her with the prow of the longboat, and Josie and Peter would have a lovely time playing the game.

She put down her coffee cup and went back into the classroom. She wasn't surprised to find the computer switched on again. She sat down nervously in front of it.

'I hope I'm doing the right thing,' she said to herself.

'Now, how do I find out if I've done any damage to the game? Ask Help, I suppose. That's what it's there for.' And she clicked on the Help icon. What she didn't know was that Francis was peering through the window, watching her.

Victor Virus responded to the summons instantly, but he was a shadow of the figure Miss Wordsworth had spoken to the night before. No sparkling smile, no shine in his eyes. He looked pale and angry.

'Good heavens!' Miss Wordsworth gasped. 'Are you supposed to look like that?'

Victor Virus managed a wan smile. 'There's a small problem in the programming. Perhaps you could help me!'

'A Help icon that needs help? How very strange! What do I have to do?'

'Type UNDO LAST COMMAND at once.'

Miss Wordsworth did as she was told. The screen went completely blank for a second and then a sickly yellow. Victor Virus reappeared, smiling so all his teeth flashed at once. He was polishing his power pen, and looked completely restored to health, as indeed he was.

'Congratulations!' he beamed. 'Complete success! Do call me any time you need help.'

The bell rang for the end of break-time, and Miss Wordsworth jumped up from the chair and went to tidy up some of the bits of tissue paper that were scattered round the floor. She felt immensely relieved. Everything was all right again and she could get on with her work.

Victor Virus gloated. 'Back to my old self again!' he sang. 'That was a near thing. Simon seems to have his heart set on zapping me. But I've got a surprise for him! Now where were we?'

He flicked his pen and stood up slowly, and as he did so his Help outfit turned into a suit of black armour.

'Sir Victor!' he laughed softly. 'The black knight of the Castle of Gloom. I can rewrite your game, Simon. I can do anything I want!'

Super-virus-buster Zzaap whizzed neatly through the vaults of the castle. He knew the little humans were around somewhere, but he was more interested in finding out whether Victor Virus had entered this level as well. If he had, he needed to be zapped before any more damage was done to the game.

He passed the children by the Wall of Spikes. They were far too busy eating to notice him and, besides, he felt sure he was on the right trail. His antennae were beginning to pick up electronic signals. Victor Virus was somewhere around.

'I need to be careful,' he buzzed to himself.

He switched off his light and entered the virus zone. The first thing he saw was the black Help suit hanging neatly in mid-air. It was still warm.

'Zip zap zee, this is serious. The virus has taken over the Help menu – which means that he must get stronger every time the outside humans make any contact. I've got to stop him now, before it's too late.'

'It's already too late,' said a soft voice behind him. 'Did you think I couldn't see you, you blue nuisance?'

Zzaap felt an acute pain in his chest. His arms and legs went numb, his wings drooped, the air went black around him, and he lost consciousness altogether.

The rusty knight cleared his throat. 'Ah! Josie and Peter! This is where I come in!'

Skinless rattled with laughter. 'It's Sir Clifford Clank. Just missed your supper!'

Sir Clifford ignored him. 'It's time for your spelling test. If you get it right you pass on to the Spirit of Stories, but if you get it wrong . . . t-r-o-u-b-l-e spells trouble!'

'Oh no. I'm useless at spelling,' Peter groaned.

'Then you'd better leave it to me,' Josie told him.

The knight cleared his throat. He was obviously enjoying this. 'First of all, what am I?'

'Are you a knight?' Josie asked. She was shaking. 'Sir?'

'What kind of a knight?'

'It might be a puzzle,' Peter suggested. 'A spelling puzzle!'

'A knight beginning with K!' Josie said. 'Easy! K-n-i-g-h-t.'

'Correct! What else begins with 'k-n'?'

Peter and Josie looked at each other wildly. 'Like what?'

'Like what he might cut your throat with,' whispered Skinless behind them.

'Knife!' said Josie.

'Excellent!' Sir Clifford smiled cheerfully at them. 'I didn't think of that one. You're jolly good at this.' He pulled a scroll out of his chainmail and consulted it. 'Give me another one.'

'Found in a rope on a hangman's noose,' Skinless whispered.

'Knot,' said Josie.

'Wonderful! I think that should do,' said Sir Clifford, rolling up his scroll. 'You can come with me now.'

But just as he turned to go, he was pushed to one side. A tall knight in black armour stood in the doorway, filling every inch of it. Skinless's bones rattled.

'Not yet!' roared the black knight. 'The boy human hasn't even opened his mouth!'

He advanced towards Peter, who tried to shrink behind Josie.

'And take no notice of claptrap here. You!' He stuck his tinny finger in Peter's chest. 'Your turn! There's a small, ugly, fat elf thing. Spell it!'

And, terrified out of his wits, Peter gasped, 'Gnome. K-n- . . .'

'No!' said Josie.

'Oo-er,' said Skinless.

'WRONG!' bellowed the black knight. 'Gnome begins with 'g-n'. Into the dungeon with you both.'

He grabbed the children by the wrists and dragged them down the stairs. He stopped outside a studded door and flung them into a dark cell.

'Stay in there till you rot!'

The Dingy Dungeon

The children ran in from the playground, red-cheeked from the fresh air. They had to swap jobs now – the designers were carpenters, the carpenters were measurers, the measurers were painters. The longboat looked wonderful. Simon followed them in, clutching his mug of coffee.

'Still with us, Simon?' Miss Wordsworth asked.

Simon looked anxiously towards the computer area. It was time to check that the virus was truly zapped.

'I thought I might hang around for a bit.'

'Great! Any good at Viking shields?'

'Erm – not really – I'm just going to check something on the computer, if that's all right.'

'Can I help him?' Francis asked.

'Five minutes!' Miss Wordsworth smiled to herself. They were going to have a nice surprise. She glanced round for Josie and Peter. No sign of them. Well, they must have gone straight to the game. 'Someone else can have a go soon.'

'Me!' said Ellie at once.

'And me,' said Tom.

'What's that word?'

'Please,' they both said, and grinned at each other excitedly. That was as good as a promise from Miss Wordsworth.

Francis reached the computer before Simon did. He was just in time to see the black knight locking the door of the dungeon and striding away, laughing horribly to himself.

'Is it going OK?' Simon asked, sitting down next to him.

'It's a bit different. Did you run the anti-virus program?'

'Of course. What d'you think I've been doing all break-time?'

'That's all right then,' Francis said. 'I was just a bit worried when I saw the black knight locking Josie and Peter in the dungeon.'

'You should trust me.' Simon yawned and stretched slowly. Then he jumped up so quickly that he knocked over his coffee, spilling it down his trousers. '*Black* knight, did you say?'

'Really evil. How did you get him to laugh like that?'

'*Black* knight!' Simon said again. He scanned the castle, flipping from screen to screen, from the dungeon right up to the tower. He shook his head, and scanned back to the dungeon. Outside, in a cobbled courtyard, stood a rusty knight. 'It's OK. It's only Sir Clifford Clank.

And he's a silver knight. He's not evil. He's just silly. Gosh – you had me worried for a moment.'

Francis frowned. It was definitely a black knight that he had seen, and there was nothing silly about him at all. 'Let me check up on Josie and Peter.'

He scanned into the dungeon. He saw Peter balancing on Josie's back to look out of the tiny slit of a window into the courtyard.

'They failed the spelling test!' he chuckled. 'Miss Wordsworth won't be pleased!'

Simon looked over his shoulder. 'Ah, but look!' He focused in on a pale blue bug lying lifeless on the cobbled floor. 'A dead virus! Now do you believe me?'

'Can you see anything?' Josie gasped. Peter was much heavier than he looked.

'There's a cobbled yard outside. There's a wall with a bird carved on it, but the head's been knocked off. And there's a real bird on a post, an owl or something, but all its feathers are dropping off and you can see its bones. It's disgusting.'

'Get down now,' Josie panted. 'You weigh a ton after all that cherry pie.'

'Wait a bit. There's that suit of armour, but I don't think there's anyone in it.'

The rusty knight clanged his shield. 'Did someone speak?'

'It's me,' Peter said. 'I'm in the dungeon.'

'Ah!' said Sir Clifford. 'That's it, Josie and Peter.' He clunked across the cobbles towards them. 'Soon get you out of there, when I find the keys.' He banged his hands down his chest and legs. 'Did have the keys. Seem to have lost them. Don't go away.' He crashed back over the cobbles and ducked through an archway, banging his head.

Peter slid off Josie's back. 'He's useless.'

'But quite harmless by the sound of him. Not like that other one,' she shuddered. 'We'll just have to sit it out till he finds the keys. If he finds them.'

The dungeon smelt musty, as if a hundred mice had died in there, and probably they had. There was nowhere to sit, except on the damp floor, but anyway they didn't feel like sitting.

'It's all my fault,' Peter said.

'You couldn't help it,' Josie said generously. 'The black knight didn't exactly give you a lot of time to think.'

A faint blue light flickered and faded again in the corner of the dungeon. Peter stared at it and then shrugged. It could have been anything. Josie went over to it.

'Hey! Look what I've found,' she cried.

'It's that bluebottle,' said Peter. 'He gets everywhere.'

'Poor Zzaap.'

'Is he dead?'

'I think so.' Josie picked Zzaap up carefully. He buzzed feebly. 'Well, nearly.'

There was a clattering as if a lot of tins had fallen over. Sir Clifford Clank peered through the slit window.

'Found the keys!' he chuckled. 'Dangling on the branch of the ash tree, where I always put them. Always forget! Trouble is, can't remember which one opens the door. You only get two chances before it seals up for ever! The Spirit of Stories is waiting for you in the Banqueting Hall, so be quick.'

He threw the bunch of keys through the slit, and they rattled across the floor. Josie knelt down, spread them out, and found that they all had letters on them. *Re.* She examined another one. *Dis.*

'They're not proper words. *Un. Dis. Re. Non,*' she said.

'Perhaps they help to make words, like *non*sense,' Peter suggested nervously.

'Peter! You're brilliant!' Josie said. Peter smiled to himself. It was the first time in his life anyone had said that to him.

Zzaap buzzed again.

'I think he's telling us you're right,' Josie said. '*Re.* We want to *re*turn to the classroom. Shall we try that one?'

She tried to push the *re* key into a hole in the door. It jammed and it was all they could do to get it out again.

'You'd better do the next one,' Josie said. 'We've only got one more chance. Don't waste it.'

Zzaap's light went out.

'*Dis.* The way out is covered up. *Dis*cover the way out,' suggested Sir Clifford from the dungeon window. 'I like *dis*. You will *dis*solve if you don't solve it! Now that is clever. You will *disappear* for ever. You will *dis*integrate! What a word! Disintegrate!' He clanged his hands together in excitement.

'Ignore him,' Josie whispered. 'He means well, but I don't think he's very bright.'

'What about *un*?' Zzaap buzzed loudly as Peter closed his hand round the *un* key. '*Un*lock!'

The key fitted perfectly. The door swung open. They stepped through as if they were in a dream, and when they turned round, it had closed up behind them.

'We've forgotten Zzaap!' wailed Josie.

'No, we haven't. I've got him. All right, Zzaap?' A faint hum came from Peter's bag.

Sir Clifford Clank was waiting for them in the corner of the yard.

'Quick, quick,' he called. 'She's been waiting too long already.'

He clattered up the winding stairs and the children ran after him. It was wonderful to be free again, and they were longing to explore the castle, but there was no time.

'Who are we meeting?' Josie asked.

'The Spirit of Stories,' Sir Clifford Clank whispered. 'Now whatever happens, don't go letting her tell you a story or you'll be here for years. Ask her who she is. In you go.'

'Found them!' said Simon. 'At last!'

'Rounders!' Miss Wordsworth called from the end of the classroom. 'Line up, everyone! Yes, I know it's cold outside, but even Viking ship builders have to play rounders!'

'But it's our turn on the computer, Miss Wordsworth,' said Ellie.

'You're next,' Miss Wordsworth promised. 'After Games. Come on, you computer buffs! Leave the game now.'

Simon raised his eyebrows at Francis.

'I'm not going now!' Francis muttered. 'We've only just found them again.'

Simon poked his head round the side of the bookshelves.

'Er . . . can we just let Josie and Peter get out of this level?' he asked. 'They're practically there. Then they can hand over to Tom and Ellie. OK?'

Miss Wordsworth was watching the other children running to the changing rooms. Ellie and Tom hung back, begging her with their eyes to let them have their turn. She shooed them on. 'I'll have a mutiny on my hands if they have to wait much longer.'

'Five minutes?'

'Five minutes,' she agreed. 'Then send them to Games.'

She followed the stragglers down the corridor and Simon sank back into his chair. Francis sighed with relief. Miss Wordsworth hadn't even noticed he wasn't with the others.

'You're not really going to let Ellie and Tom play are you? Francis asked. 'The same thing might happen to them!'

'No way,' said Simon. 'If she mentions it again you'll just have to think of something to keep her distracted. Pretend you can't do your maths or something.'

'But I can always do my maths.'

Simon shook his head and turned back to the screen. 'Now, where were we?'

The Spirit of Stories

They stepped into a vaulted hall that was lit by hundreds of candles. By the fire sat a beautiful woman with long black hair and dark eyes. Her skin was dusky gold. She was dressed in golden robes and veils studded with jewels that flashed like stars.

'Ah, Peter and Josie, I have been waiting for you. Come and sit by the fire, and let me tell you a story. Once upon a . . .'

'No, thank you,' said Peter.

'Don't you like stories?' asked the beautiful woman, sad and surprised.

'Yes,' said Josie. 'But not just now.'

'Once upon a time, in a certain city –'

'What's your name?' Josie interrupted her.

'My name?' The beautiful woman stared at her with her deep, dark-brown eyes, and then she began to sing, very softly, and as she sang her jewels and sequins cast sparks like fire into all the shadowy corners of the hall.

'I am the Spirit of Stories,' she sang, and the letter S floated out of her lips like a bubble of light. 'I am the Caster of spells. I Have the words to make wondErs, and Horrors that nobody tells. I can Enchant you with

*R*hyming, I can *A*ma*Z*e you with song, I can make *A*ll things happen, give you *D*reams to last all day long. But there is no *E*nd to my stories, till one thousand and one nights have passed. Tell me my name and my secret, and you will have freedom at last.'

Bubbles were dancing all round her, lit up by the sparks from her jewels, and the letters inside every bubble glowed green, or gold, or blue. Peter caught the bubbles one by one and they burst in his hand. He laid out the letters on the stone hearth in front of the fire.

'SCHEHERAZADE,' he wrote. 'There. I'm sure I've got all the letters in the right order, but I can't say it.'

'It's Scheherazade,' said Josie, who wasn't sure herself how to say it. 'Miss Wordsworth told us about her! She had to tell the Sultan a story every night, for a thousand and one nights, or he'd kill her.'

Scheherazade laughed, a wonderful musical laugh like the sound of flutes playing. 'You've earned the right to leave the Castle,' she said. 'But surely you have time for a story first.'

'Yes, please,' said Josie. 'I love stories. Could you tell me the one about Aladdin and his magic lamp? And then Sinbad?'

Scheherazade leaned back against her cushions. Her sequin lights danced around the walls. 'Once upon a time, in a certain city in China . . .' she began. Peter took Zzaap out of his bag and showed him to her.

'We can't stay,' he said. 'I've got a very sick bug here.' Zzaap stirred slightly. 'He needs some proper medicine.'

'Oh, what a sad story that would make! Take him to my friend, the Guardian of the Green Glen,' said Scheherazade. She glided over to a tapestry. 'He lives far away from the Castle of Gloom. You must go to nowhere

65

and look for the point where two opposites meet. There
your freedom lies. But if you'd like to stay here for about
three years, I could tell you a story every night.'

As she was speaking, her voice was growing fainter.
She faded slowly into the tapestry until she had
disappeared completely. Peter ran up to the tapestry and
touched it, and lines and words scribbled themselves over
the surface.

'It looks like a map,' said Josie.

'It is. It's a map of the castle. Look – there's the
dungeon, and there's the Wall of Spikes.'

'The spiral staircase. And this is the Banqueting Hall.'

'So where's the point where two opposites meet?'

'Look outside,' buzzed Zzaap, so faintly that he sounded like the flickering of candles.

'Right. Outside.' Peter traced round the grounds of the castle on the map. 'It's cut off on that side by two streams. It's hard to read this squiggly writing. One's called the Stream of Sorrow – and the other one is the Stream of Joy. They're opposites, aren't they?'

'And the point where they meet –' Josie traced the routes with her finger, 'Oh, Peter. It's under the Bridge to Nowhere.'

The great studded door swung open and the fluttering lights of the torches on the walls began to grow dim.

'Goodbye, Cherryade,' said Peter.

'Goodbye, Scheherazade,' corrected Josie.

They ran to the staircase, past the Wall of Spikes. Skinless raised his hand and grinned at them.

'Woe is me! Such weeping and wailing! What would I wager for a wee something to wet my whistle!'

'He means he's thirsty. Water!' Josie shouted, not stopping. 'Wine!'

'Whisky!' giggled Peter on his way past.

'Water will do fine! There's plenty of that where you're going.'

'Left, right,' the heads called.

Their voices echoed round the spiral staircase as the children raced down and out into the cobbled yard of the castle, past the post with the skeleton owl and up to

the Bridge to Nowhere. There on the bridge stood Sir
Clifford Clank, his lance tilted to bar their way.

'Passwords!' he shouted. 'Awfully sorry. Or you have
to stay in the Castle of Gloom for ever. What do you
want, a blessing or a curse?'

Peter and Josie looked at each other.

'Opposites,' whispered Peter. 'The puzzle.'

'Sorrow and joy!' shouted Josie.

Sir Clifford stepped aside, beaming at them.

'That's it. They're free! They're on the Bridge to
Nowhere!' said Simon.

'Brilliant! Phew!'

'Off you go to Games. I'll come and watch for a bit.'

He and Francis both stood up and left the computer.
They could see that Peter and Josie were quite safe, that
was the main thing. They both felt a bit shaky by now,
in need of a stretch and a bit of fresh air.

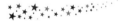

But Peter and Josie weren't safe, not by any means.
A black figure appeared on the castle ramparts, glaring
down at them.

'Stop those humans!' he roared. 'They're mine!' His
voice echoed round the courtyard.

'It's the black knight,' Peter gasped.

They pounded along the bridge. It creaked and
swayed beneath them, and then came to a halt. The

bridge stopped in mid-air. Its two support posts sank down into a frothing pool where two rivers met, boiling and churning like a cauldron of oil.

'It doesn't go anywhere!' Josie said. 'That's why it's called the Bridge to Nowhere!'

They turned round. The black knight was striding across the cobbled yard towards them. He thrust Sir Clifford Clank to one side as if he were nothing but a pile of tin cans.

'You have nowhere to go!' he laughed. 'You're mine now. Mine!'

'What are we going to do?' Josie asked. Her voice fluttered like a moth.

The black knight strode down the bridge.

'There's only one thing we can do,' said Peter. He grabbed her hand and turned back to the end of the bridge. 'Jump!'

They closed their eyes and jumped. Peter's bag flapped open and out tumbled Zzaap, pale and lifeless, and disappeared into the foaming spray.

Level three

ETH NEGL FO HET REGEN NAM

Lord Hamish Crow

Just when it seemed that they would be dashed to pieces on the rocks below, Peter grabbed hold of a tree, or rather it grabbed him, and he snatched at Josie's sweatshirt and managed to pull her with him into the shelter of the tree roots.

And the day suddenly turned bright. A deer was watching them from a glen below and the sun was shining. Flowers bloomed. Butterflies flitted everywhere and the air was full of birdsong. It was a perfect summer's day.

Victor Virus snarled. 'Lost them! After all that, those humans have escaped again. Well, how clever they are. Just what I need! And I will catch them.'

He flicked his power pen and metamorphosed out of his black knight armour into a wetsuit. He drew a pool of water around him, pinched his nose, and dived.

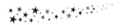

'Thank you for saving me,' said Josie.

'I didn't. It was the tree.'

The tree creaked peacefully. It seemed to have creatures nestling into every hole and crack. Whenever they looked, everything seemed to grow still again, and to change its colour and texture so it appeared to melt right into the tree.

'I think this is a magic place,' Josie whispered, and the old tree rustled its leaves and whispered back to her.

'It is. It's the Green Glen. If you're lucky you'll see the Guardian.'

'Cherryade told us about him!' Peter said. 'We've got to see him, to ask him to make Zzaap better – oh! Zzaap! Oh no!'

He put his hand in his bag. All the letters and pebbles he'd picked up and saved were there, but there was no Zzaap.

'He's drowned!'

'Oh, your little friend will be all right,' chuckled the tree. 'Nothing comes to any harm in the Green Glen. Everybody helps everybody here, you see. For instance, somebody needs your help right now. You find a way of helping him, and he might find a way of helping you.'

'Help!' came a voice. 'Could somebody lend me a wing please?' It was a Scottish voice, rather grand. A crow shook spray from its feathers. 'Help!'

'What's the matter?' asked Josie.

The crow gasped and bubbled like an old kettle on the boil. 'Can't you see? I'm trying to get over this waterfall, and it keeps pushing me down again. I used to be able to do it. I can't understand it.' He flapped about wearily. 'Ah, I see you're having a wee breather too. How did you get here, might I ask?'

'We just kind of fell, and slid, and landed,' said Peter. 'But we were trying to go down, not up. It must be much harder going up.'

'Och, it is, it is! But there is a way, if only I can find the right word for it. I've forgotten it. It's an 'ily' word.'

'A silly word?' Peter laughed. He felt so happy here in the sunshine that nothing seemed to be worth worrying about. 'Like – bolobble! Or – solausages!' He took off his shoes and socks and dibbled them in the water.

'I see no reason to laugh,' the crow grumped. 'An 'l-y' word. It's on the tip of my beak. Give me an 'l-y' word.'

'I think I know what he means.' Josie stretched lazily. 'He wants to play the adverb game.'

'Never heard of it,' yawned Peter.

'My dear child. I am Lord Hamish Crow, the oldest and wisest bird in the glen. I do not,' he snapped his beak, 'play games.'

'Fly happily over the waterfall,' suggested Peter. 'Go on. Try it.'

Lord Hamish croaked to show his disapproval. 'I am not much given to doing anything happily.' He attempted to laugh. 'Ha-ha! Ha-ha! He-he!' He gave a mighty leap and reached about half-way up the waterfall. Then he flopped down again into a rock pool, splashing both the children. 'Not bad,' he muttered, a little bit embarrassed. 'But not quite right.'

'Try jumping sadly up the waterfall.'

'Boo-hoo. That won't be hard.' He sniffed miserably and gave a sorry little jump. It hardly got him anywhere.

'Grumpily,' suggested Josie. 'That should suit him . . .'

'Splendidly. No. Naughtily. No good. Bravely. Hurriedly. No.'

It all caused a lot of flapping and the children laughed a lot, but Lord Hamish was growing crosser by the minute.

'I am pleased to be causing you some amusement, but I am extremely tired and no nearer the top of the waterfall than I ever was. And it's well past eleven o'clock by now, may I remind you,' he said politely. 'If you want to talk to the Guardian today, and you want to find your wee friend . . .'

The children sat, thinking hard. Then Josie said, 'I don't

think we should be asking Lord Hamish to do anything that isn't natural to him. It's easy for a crow to fly.'

Lord Hamish nodded. 'It used to be so easy for me in my youth. I was the finest bird in the glen, you know . . .'

'OK, we've heard all that,' said Josie quickly. 'This is what I think you should do. Fly *easily* over the waterfall, Lord Hamish.'

'Easily.' He opened his beak as if he were swallowing the word like a live fly, and he soared up and up, out of the water, with his feathers gleaming in the sunshine.

'My, oh my!' he crowed. 'How easy it is! What a shame you're not birds too! Thank you my wee friends. Thank you!' And he disappeared over the crest of the waterfall.

'But wait!' Peter shouted. 'You were going to tell us where to find the Guardian of the Green Glen.' But Lord Hamish had gone.

* * * * * * * * * * *

Half-dressed for Games, Francis came running down the corridor, colliding into Simon.

'What's up?' asked Simon. 'I thought you were going to rounders?'

'I've just seen Miss Wordsworth going back to the classroom. What if she looks at the computer? It's still on!'

'I'll be right with you. Go and distract her for a minute. I've left my note-book somewhere.'

'What shall I say?'

'I don't know – tell her about that dog in the playground.'

'What dog?' But Simon had gone back into the staff room. He might be allowed there, but Francis certainly wasn't. He ran back to the classroom. Sure enough, he found Miss Wordsworth sweeping round the computer area, picking up bits of string and cardboard again. She had just straightened up and was staring idly at the screen when Francis came charging in.

'Miss Wordsworth, Simon says there's a dog in the playground. A big dog,' he added, trying to impress her.

'Oh dear.' She looked worried. 'Then you'd better tell the caretaker.'

'Not very big,' he reassured her. 'Normal size, really.'

'Oh, well I'll see to it.'

He watched her go out of the classroom and down the corridor and then ran back to the computer, scanning for Josie and Peter again.

'Where are you, where are you?' he muttered, and then he found them having a lovely time paddling and splashing under the waterfall.

'Lucky lollipops!' he sighed. 'They're in the Green Glen. And it looks really hot there too. What's that in the water?'

Josie tapped Peter's arm and pointed down to the pool. There was a piece of paper floating in the water. She picked it out and, as it dried, words began to appear on it:

Trust the word of the noble lord,
Find soldiers with neither gun nor sword

Where the captain is rooted to the ground
The path to the eye of land is found.

The old tree rustled her leaves over their heads.

'The sun is nearly at its height,' she whispered.

Josie stretched lazily and glanced at the piece of paper again. Peter looked over her shoulder.

'I don't even know who the noble lord is,' he said.

'Oh, that bit's easy,' said Josie. 'Lord Hamish Crow, of course. This is a message from him. But soldiers?' She gazed round her. 'There are no soldiers here, and I wouldn't want to find them if there were.'

'Neither gun nor sword,' Peter said. 'That means they're not fighting soldiers. Perhaps they just look like soldiers. What looks like a soldier?'

He stood up, shielding his eyes with his hands because the sun was so bright. And he heard, very faint on the breeze, someone shouting, 'Left, right, left, right, about turn, quick march.'

Coming up the side of the river was a column of trees, their trunks so tall and straight that it seemed as if their heads were in the sky.

'Halt!' the voice cried, and the trees stopped marching and stood perfectly still.

'There's our soldiers. Of course. Find where the captain is rooted to the ground – so we look for the most important one – and find our path.'

The oak tree rustled her leaves again. 'You must guess the name of the Guardian.'

Josie and Peter patted her trunk to say goodbye, and

ran down to where the soldier trees were drawing up their shadows. And there, sure enough, they found that one of the trees was much taller and straighter than any of the others. They stood underneath its branches and consulted the message. *The path to the eye of land is found.* A path snaked away through the bluebells to the banks of a river.

'Now what?' asked Peter. A tree on the river bank turned into a signpost with a flashing green man pointing to an island in the middle of the river. 'The eye of the land! An island! Oh wow, I'm good at puzzles after all!'

The river was shallow at this point. Little bright fish flashed around their legs as they splashed across.

'Hey, they're not real fish! They're letters,' Peter said, and he laid them out on the island shore to dry. REGEN NAM.

Blue Light Undoes Enemy

'Well, where's this Guardian we're supposed to be looking for?' Josie started searching the island while Peter played with the fish letters.

'I can make two words out of them!' he called. 'GREEN and MAN.'

'Green man,' said Josie slowly, staring at a bush. 'Green man.' She was sure she could see a pair of bright eyes smiling out at her from among the leaves. 'It's the Green Man!' she said again. 'That's his name!'

And out sprang a man who was clothed from head to toe in leaves; leaves in his hair, leaves sprouting from his ears and bracelets of green berries and plaited vines on his wrists. His eyes were as green as grass. He frisked round them, leaping in and out of bushes so it was hard to tell which was him and which was foliage.

'I am king of the budding spring, I can bring life to anything,' he sang in a reedy, piping voice. 'Yes?' He sat cross-legged on the grass, waiting for them to speak.

'Erm. Cherryade told us about you,' Peter said.

'Scheherazade,' said Josie.

'Mmm. And we wanted Zzaap to be made better – but – we've lost him.'

The Green Man flicked his long fingers. 'Is this your friend?' he asked. 'His life was nearly at an end.'

Zzaap appeared in a shimmering green light.

'Zzaap! You're well again!' said Josie.

Zzaap buzzed moodily round their heads. 'I'm very well, thank you. But you might have noticed that I'm the wrong colour.'

The Green Man danced round them. 'Green is the perfect colour. How can it be the wrong colour? It is the colour of trees and grass and leaves – it is the colour of life itself.'

'Yes, but it isn't my colour. I look like a greenfly. Do something.'

'I think I preferred him when he was zapped!' Peter whispered to Josie. 'I'd forgotten how annoying he is.'

'You have to see it from his point of view. Would you want to be green?'

'No,' Peter admitted. 'But I wouldn't want to be blue either.'

Zzaap whizzed up to them. 'Stop whispering and do something to help me, or we'll never be out of this place. I have to guide you through the glen, and you'll never even see me if I'm green! There's more levels to go yet, you know, before you reach the Word Master. Do you want me to help you or not?'

It was obvious that he wasn't at all happy, but the Green Man wasn't happy either.

'Nothing is more beautiful than green. Blue is very scarce,' he shook his head. 'I have to dig out the heart of a glacier for that. You'll have to give me a very good reason for being blue before I can do anything.'

Zzaap sighed. 'I have a very good reason. You don't know who I am, do you?'

They all shook their heads.

'I am the super-cyber-hero Zzaap!'

They shook their heads again.

'My mission here is to destroy the virus who is ruining this game. He got you into this mess, in case you didn't know, and I'm trying to get you out of it and out of his power.'

'Is he the black knight?' Josie asked.

'He's whoever he wants to be. He's Victor Virus, and he's the nastiest virus I've come across. My blue light is my only weapon against him. His weapon is yellow, and believe me, it's got a sting! And he picks up more power every time he makes contact with one of your outside humans.'

'How does he do that?' asked Peter, amazed. A virus communicating with school! Surely nobody would talk to a virus!

'He can take any shape he wants,' Zzaap explained. 'And sometimes he pretends to a be a nice friendly Help icon. I found his suit. In the Castle of Gloom he pretended to be a black knight. He didn't bother with charm that time, though – straight into mean mode.'

'We noticed,' Josie said. 'I couldn't believe Simon had invented anyone so horrible.'

'Well, now you see what we're up against? I can't zap him without my blue light. Blue Light Undoes Enemy.'

He zipped round them, flashing his green light on and off, and buzzing with annoyance.

'B-L-U-E. See? And don't ask me to spell anything else. That's the only word I can do, apart from Z-z-a-a-p. That's me! Green's no good. Sorry, Green Man. Green's useless to me!' He sank down into a pile of leaves, slumping so he practically disappeared from sight. He was fed up.

'Green Man, is there anything we can do?' Josie asked.

The Green Man closed his eyes. He looked as if he were deeply hurt, or maybe he had even gone to sleep. Josie looked at Peter and motioned him with her hand to keep still. They heard a faint rustling, like the sound reeds make in the wind. It was the Green Man singing softly to himself.

'I will pour the blue of glaciers into my green wilderness. I will take the scent of bluebells and the breath of bluebirds, the song of blue whales, the taste of blueberries. I will drain the blue from the sky and from the deepest oceans.'

For a moment everything turned dark, as though the moon had eclipsed the sun, and then flooded with light again. Zzaap rose up into the air as bright as a dragon-fly.

'Zip zap zee, I'm me again! Oh blue, blue, beautiful blue!' And out of sheer joy he did several perfect somersaults.

Miss Wordsworth rapped on the classroom window. Francis nearly jumped out of his skin.

'I want you out here this minute!' she mouthed.

When he arrived in the playground, Francis could see that she was not at all pleased with him.

'What are you up to, Francis?' she demanded. 'There's no dog in this yard – not even a medium-sized one. And what were you doing in the classroom anyway? You were supposed to be at Games.'

'Yes, Miss Wordsworth.' He'd forgotten all about that dog. Anyway, it was Simon's idea.

Miss Wordsworth softened. 'I know you love Simon's game, but there are other games too – like rounders.'

'Yes, Miss Wordsworth.'

'So get some fresh air and leave that computer alone.'

'Yes, Miss Wordsworth. Do you like rounders, Miss Wordsworth?' Silly question really, but he had to keep her away from the classroom until Simon came back.

'Mmm. I used to be quite good at it – off you go, Francis. I've told Ellie and Tom they can play straight after Games – on their own, mind!'

'Yes, Miss Wordsworth.'

'By the way – where are Josie and Peter? Any idea? They aren't on that playing field. Find them, please.'

Francis edged off towards the playing field and then, as soon as Miss Wordsworth turned, ran back to the classroom.

'I'm glad you're better, Zzaap,' Josie said, even though he was being noisy and annoying again, zipping round her head and singing loudly. 'I didn't realise you were so important.'

'Well, now you know who I am you'd better tell your outside people too. I don't want them thinking that I'm the one causing all the trouble round here. I don't

84

belong in this game, I only came in to sort out the problem. But if anyone's watching they're going to see me and try and rub me out or something.' He shivered. 'And I've had enough of that. And what would happen to you, without me here to protect you?'

'Leave Zzaap alone. He's not a virus!' Josie shouted, waving her arms about.

Zzaap buzzed impatiently. 'It's no good shouting. I don't know whether they can hear you.'

They slumped down. They had to think about this. It had never occurred to them that someone might be sitting in the classroom actually watching them.

'They might try to delete us too!' Peter whispered. The thought of being watched from outside the game was really strange.

'I know what to do,' Josie said suddenly. 'But you'll all have to help. I need lots of leaves and twigs.'

'I hope you're not going to hurt them,' the Green Man said. 'Especially the new young leaves. You'd better leave this to me.' He whisked his arms around and sent a breeze scurrying like a mouse round the island, bringing back with it little yellow and brown clouds of old dead leaves that had been lying under the trees.

'Right.' Josie scooped up an armload. 'Follow me.'

Simon was walking down the corridor when Francis panted up to him.

'Everything's going wrong.'

He looked so mournful and exhausted that Simon wished he had a chocolate biscuit for him. 'Like what?'

Francis told him the worst thing first – that he'd seen the blue bug again. 'Only he's turned green now.'

'Impossible,' Simon said. 'I zapped him.'

'Well, he's come back. Or maybe it's another one. And that's not all. Miss Wordsworth says Tom and Ellie have to play now.'

Simon shook his head. 'Well, they can't. It's not safe. Heaven knows what might happen to them if they do.'

'And she knows Josie and Peter aren't at rounders. She's looking for them. What can we do?'

Simon deliberated. 'Leave it to me. You've done your best, but there's nothing else you can do.'

Francis went trudging mournfully down the corridor as if he had the weight of the whole world on his shoulders. Simon watched him and sighed. He knew there was nothing more he could do either.

'Face the music,' he told himself. 'It's time I confessed to Miss Wordsworth.'

By the time Francis finished changing for Games, the rounders game was finished and everyone was coming back in. Ellie and Tom were running in front, keen to get straight back to the classroom.

'It's us now!' Ellie called. 'Our turn on *Word Master*!'

Francis tried to block their way. 'Hey, I wouldn't play it if I were you.'

Tom laughed at him. 'Think we're not clever enough?'

'Something horrible might happen to you.'

'Like what?' said Ellie scornfully. 'Meeting the Word Master? I'm not scared of him.'

Tom tried to push his way past. 'Just because you didn't get that far.'

'No, honestly. It's not safe!' Francis felt desperate. Tom and Ellie looked at each other. They'd never seen Francis looking so worried. 'If you don't believe me, you'd better ask Josie and Peter.' And, out of the blue, he had the best idea that day. 'Come on, ask them.'

In the Green Glen, Josie was organising Peter, Zzaap and the Green Man into spreading out all the leaves and twigs they'd collected onto the path. Then she and Peter arranged them into letters.

'What are they doing?' Zzaap asked.

'I think it's what humans call writing,' said the Green Man wisely.

'I know that!' Zzaap buzzed. 'But what does it say? Can't you read?'

'I can read very well,' the Green Man answered proudly. 'But not human language. I'm a bit ahead of them, you see.'

'There!' Josie said, when she and Peter had finished. 'That should do it.'

'OK, OK. Great,' Zzaap zipped along the letters,

mouthing words as though he were trying to read. 'Now, let's get out of here quickly. You never know who might be lurking. Into the trees while we decide what we must do next.'

And so they were too late to see the surface of the river bubbling and frothing and a black shape rising out of it. It was a man in a wet suit. As he lifted off his hood, he heard the sound of Zzaap buzzing. Then he saw a blue light flickering through the trunks of the trees.

'That interfering insect!' he snarled. 'That pesky parasite! I thought I'd got rid of him once!'

He clambered up onto the path, flapping his flippers like a duck, and peeled off his goggles. Now he could see clearly, up on the hillside, the message that Josie and Peter had written. And, unlike Zzaap and the Green Man, he could read it.

'So. Clever little humans, eh? But not as clever as me!' As he was speaking, he was shedding his black suit, metamorphosing into something quite different.

The Good Guy Guide

Miss Wordsworth was warming her hands on the radiator when the children streamed into class.

'Hurry, hurry,' she called. 'I'm sure the Vikings were never late back from Games! We've got a longboat to finish you know. I think we'll be crossing the North Sea soon.'

As she was speaking, she was looking for Josie and Peter. They must have slipped past her to the computer again.

'Come on, you two!' she said, going round behind the bookshelves. Funny. No sign of them. Then she saw the strange message written in twigs and leaves on the computer screen.

'Do not zap zzaap. Zzaap is not the virus,' she read. 'What's that supposed to mean?'

She glanced behind her. The children had all settled into their tasks. She sat down and clicked on the Help icon. Immediately, Victor Virus appeared, neat and shining in his suit. A yellow pen flashed in his pocket.

'Do you need help?' he asked, smiling like sunshine.

'I don't know. I don't understand the message.'

'It's incorrect, that's why. You must delete both the *not* words. I repeat. Delete both the *not* words immediately.' He dislodged his smile slightly in his earnestness.

'OK, OK.' She moved the cursor, highlighted both the *not* words in the message, and deleted them both. She leaned back in the chair, pleased with herself.

'Excellent,' Victor Virus beamed. His pen glowed. He breathed on it and polished it lovingly. And then he disappeared.

'I must tell Simon about last night,' Miss Wordsworth thought. 'He ought to know, even if all the problems are over now.' She turned round just as he came into the computer area. She saw that his face was white with worry, and knew for sure that she had to explain what had happened.

'Miss Wordsworth –' he began.

'Simon!' She took a deep breath. 'I've got something to tell you.'

'I've got something to tell you. You'd better sit down again,' he said. 'Miss Wordsworth. This is going to be a bit of a shock.'

'I love the Green Glen,' Josie said, yawning beautifully. 'It's so sunny and pretty.'

'Can't stay here, move on, move on,' Zzaap buzzed. 'If you don't move through the levels you'll never reach the Word Master, and I can't zap Victor Virus until you do.'

Josie and Peter started to paddle across the river away from the island. Zzaap skipped in the air behind them.

'Thank you, Green Man,' Josie said. 'You've helped us a lot.'

'I've done as much as I can,' he said, drawing weeping willow leaves around him like a curtain. 'Time for my sleep.'

Peter looked back at the message. 'Do not zap Zzaap. Zzaap is not the virus,' he read. 'I hope someone's looking at it.' He waved his arms about and pointed to it. 'Please, please look.'

Miss Wordsworth hesitated, then sat down. Simon could see the screen now behind her shoulder. He frowned. Not more problems!

'Do zap Zzaap. Zzaap is the virus,' he read out loud. 'What's that supposed to mean?'

'That's what I was trying to tell you. If you're having problems with the game, it might be my fault. I meant to tell you before – I was here last night – and I had a go at the game. I wanted to be able to help Peter if he got stuck. But the fact is, I got a bit confused –' She stopped. How was she going to tell him that she thought she had run a virus into his game? She tried to start again, but he interrupted her.

'It's much worse than you think.' In the classroom behind them someone fell over someone else. There was a gale of squabbling. They both ignored it. 'You're never going to believe this. Josie and Peter . . . Josie and Peter are inside the game.'

Miss Wordsworth stared at him, and then started to laugh. 'I nearly believed you for a minute!'

His face didn't change. Miss Wordsworth felt herself going cold. 'What are you telling me, Simon?'

'I'm serious. You'd better look.'

He sat down in the seat next to her and scanned through the game. And there she saw two little figures splashing through the river. Josie and Peter, as clear as anything, tiny little perfect figures in their grey school sweatshirts. Peter turned and pointed at something, danced up and down, waved his arms about, and then splashed after Josie and scrambled up on to the river bank.

'Oh, my goodness me! How did they get there?'

'I don't honestly know,' Simon admitted, 'but that seems to be what this message is about.' He looked at the computer screen again. 'Do zap Zzaap. Zzaap is the virus. I think Zzaap must be the name of that little blue bug that keeps cropping up all over the place.' He started typing computer equations. Miss Wordsworth watched him, still numb with shock.

'So what do we do now?' she asked. 'Ring the police or something – but what can they do? What can anyone do?'

'I think the only chance for them is to work through the levels of the game.' He turned round to her, pleading. 'Just let's see what happens when they reach the Word Master.' He turned back to his machine, typing rapidly, his fingers making urgent little tapping sounds on the keys.

'All right. But when their parents come for them at half past three, we'll have to tell them.'

Simon nodded. He was frowning, concentrating hard

on calculations that Miss Wordsworth couldn't begin to understand. She stood up, wringing her hands.

'I'm going to tell the class,' she decided. 'Whatever happens, they mustn't touch this machine.'

'Good idea,' he murmured, not looking up. 'Yes. Tell the others.' He stopped typing with a flourish and wiped his face on his handkerchief, which wasn't very clean. 'There! I've done what they told us to do. I've zapped Zzaap.'

Zzaap spiralled slowly down and lay on the ground. Peter ran to him and picked him up. Zzaap lay lifeless in his hand.

'Green Man!' he shouted. 'Help! Zzaap's fainted!'

'I'm sorry,' the Green Man emerged sleepily from his willow tree. 'There's nothing more I can do.'

Peter sat down on the path, nursing Zzaap, nearly in tears. Josie came and sat by him.

'Zzaap, Zzaap,' Peter whispered.

Zzaap was growing paler and weaker. He was nearly dead. Peter put him gently on the grass, hoping the warmth of the sun might make him feel better.

Just when it seemed that there was no hope left, they heard someone whistling brightly and a park ranger came striding round the bend of the path.

'Josie and Peter!' He waved to them cheerfully. 'Found you at last!'

'That's the one!' Zzaap murmured. 'It's him.' His voice faded away to nothing.

'He's trying to tell us something!' Peter said urgently.

The man was full of kind, reassuring smiles. 'Never
fear – help is here!' he chuckled. 'I've come to show you
the way out.'

'Who are you?' Peter asked doubtfully. There was
something about the man's voice that he recognised.

The man beamed down at them both. He certainly
looked friendly. 'I'm your Good Guy Guide. Simon and
Miss Wordsworth sent me to bring you home!'

'It worked!' Josie shouted. 'Our message worked!
I knew it would!'

'Don't trust him!' Zzaap whispered. Peter crouched down, but Zzaap's voice was so faint that he couldn't hear him any more. The Good Guy Guide poked him with his walking stick.

'My word, he nearly led you astray, that little bug!' He bent down, picked Zzaap up, and threw him away.

'But he's our friend!' gasped Peter.

'Friend!' the Good Guy Guide laughed. 'He's a V.D.F – Virus Disguised as Friend! The worst sort. No, if you'd followed him he'd have led you into terrible danger. Good job I arrived when I did, eh? Not that he's much danger to anyone at the moment. Come on, forget about him now. Follow me.'

Peter gazed at Zzaap. 'But we can't just leave him!'

'What use is he! A squashed fly, that's all he is. Come with me.' He smiled kindly at them. 'Trust me. I'm your friend.'

Across the river, on the island, the Green Man was watching what was going on. 'They mustn't leave Zzaap,' he said to the willow tree. 'They're the only ones who can help him now.'

The Good Guy Guide was beginning to walk away. He held his hand out to Josie, but she was looking at Zzaap too. He was hardly breathing now.

'I don't know what to do,' she said.

'Miss Wordsworth's waiting,' the Good Guy Guide said.

'Peter? What do you think?'

Peter shook his head.

'How else can we get out of here?' she asked.

The Good Guy Guide made a great show of opening up his rucksack. 'Let's see what I've got in here for you!' He brought out a map, a compass, a water bottle and a slab of chocolate-covered Kendal mint cake and held them out to Josie. She took them, smiling. It was all right. He was going to look after them, she could see that.

'Come on, Peter,' she said. 'I'm sure it's all right. How would he know Miss Wordsworth's name?'

Peter was terribly torn. He joined her reluctantly, turning back every now and again to look at the pale Zzaap, who still seemed to be trying to tell them something. The Good Guy Guide handed Peter some mint cake. His yellow pen flashed in the sunshine.

'Don't worry about the insect,' he smiled. 'You're safe now.' And he set off at a quick marching pace, and Josie skipped behind him.

'Where are you taking us, Good Guy Guide?' she asked, her mouth full of mint cake. It was delicious. It reminded her of camping holidays in the Lake District.

The Good Guy Guide paused for a moment and gazed into the distance.

'We're going to a place I'm very fond of,' he told her. 'It's called No Hope Valley.'

Aabbq jt opu uif wjsvt. Ep opu abq Aabbq.

Miss Wordsworth went back into the classroom. The children who had been squabbling went very still. They could see by her face that something serious had happened. She smiled weakly at them.

'I've got something to tell you,' she began. 'Something strange has happened. Hasn't it, Simon?'

He came round the shelves to join her. He looked at all the eager, bright faces, at the mess of cardboard, paper and string lying round, at the beautiful Viking longboat that was emerging. They were having such a nice time, he thought. And they were about to hear something so frightening that they would probably have nightmares about it for the rest of their lives. Maybe it would be better not to tell them after all. But Miss Wordsworth went on quietly.

'Something has happened to Josie and Peter.'

'Is it something to do with the game?' Matthew asked.

Miss Wordsworth nodded. 'Exactly. They are – inside Simon's game!'

There was a pause, and then the truth dawned on them. Their faces lit up. Matthew spoke for all of them. 'Ah wow! Brilliant! The lucky things!'

The Good Guy Guide was striding towards some stepping stones. Josie and Peter had to run to keep up with him.

'Is No Hope Valley the next level?' Josie asked. 'Do we have to solve a puzzle to get there?'

The Good Guy Guide paused. 'A puzzle? Ah yes, a puzzle!' He laughed. 'We have to cross the river without getting our feet wet. That's a puzzle.'

'It's not much of a puzzle,' Josie said. 'We just use the stepping stones.' She jumped on to the first one, balancing herself by stretching one arm out to the side and holding on to her hair with the other.

But Peter was still upset. He stood on the bank and refused to follow.

'We're going to get on very well,' said the Good Guy Guide. 'Come on, Peter. Don't get left behind.'

Reluctantly, Peter stepped over the stones. A mist closed round them like the breath of horses, and they simply disappeared.

The Green Man was standing under the willow tree, watching until he couldn't see them any longer.

'I've never seen him before,' he said. 'He is not to be trusted. Oh no, if I know anything at all under the sun and the moon and the stars, it is that he is not to be trusted. And how can poor Zzaap help them now? All the outside humans want to do is to drain his power away.'

'Send them a message,' the tree whispered. 'Like the little humans did.'

'Useless, Willow. They zapped him anyway. And I can't write in their language.'

Willow's leaves trickled slowly down like tears. 'Green Man, think of something. The little humans came to you for help. Don't let them down.'

The Green Man went back to the message that Josie and Peter had written. He knew what it was supposed to say, but it didn't look right to him. He made the twigs and sticks whirl and scurry like a flock of birds, and when they settled down again they looked completely different.

'Aabbq jt opu uif wjsvt. Ep opu abq aabbq,' he read.
'There! Oh, that's much better! A message for clever
people to read.'

The children scrambled excitedly into the computer
area. Miss Wordsworth and Simon were doing their
best to keep them away from the keyboard. 'Don't
touch anything!' they kept saying.

'I can't see Josie or Peter!' Wendy said, disappointed.
'Where are they supposed to be?'

'I knew it wasn't true!' Matthew said.

'Well, it is true,' Miss Wordsworth assured him. 'I've
seen them for myself. You'd better show them, Simon.'

Simon was already scanning through the Green
Glen level. 'I'm looking for them now. There's the
waterfall. There's Tree. There's the soldier trees. There's
the eye of land. There's the Green Man.'

'Oh yes!' said Oliver. 'I can see his eyes in the
willow tree.'

'And there's some funny writing on that hill,' said
Matthew.

Simon scanned into it. 'So there is. Weird!'

'It doesn't make sense,' Matthew said. 'Is it a
foreign language?'

'I've no idea what it means,' Simon told him.

'You must do! You wrote the game!'

'Write it down someone, and see if we can work it
out,' Miss Wordsworth said. 'It could be important.'

She looked at the clock. 'That time already! You'd better get off to dinner.'

'Miss!' There was a disappointed chorus. 'We haven't seen Josie and Peter yet.'

'You must go. All of you. Don't say a word to anyone else though, promise me. Not till we decide what to do.'

They all promised, wide-eyed and solemn.

'It's our secret. And it's very, very important. Right! Off you go now – Francis's group first. Annie, Wendy, Oliver – off you go.' Miss Wordsworth stood up suddenly. 'Just a minute, you others. Someone's missing. Simon –' she turned round to him, white with horror. 'It's Ellie and Tom! I sent them in from Games to play on the computer. Where are they?'

Level ~~four~~

YELLAV
EPOH ON

The bargain

Josie and Peter trudged behind the Good Guy Guide. They were in a deep, stony valley that was completely bare of trees and grass. There were no flowers, no birds or butterflies, and everything was the same dull grey – the sky, the stones, the track. The sides of the valley rose up in levels, and seemed to press down and block out any hope of sunshine. A cold wind howled like a hungry wolf around them.

'I'm really tired,' Peter complained. 'We don't seem to be getting anywhere.'

'Can't we just have a bit of a rest, Good Guy?' Josie called.

'Don't trail behind,' he called over his shoulder. 'We've got a long way to go yet.'

'I can't go any further,' Peter said stubbornly. 'I'm too tired.'

'So am I. I don't like this place.' Josie gazed round at the bleak landscape. 'There's nowhere to have any fun.'

The Good Guy Guide paused for a fraction of a second. 'Fun, did you say? Fun? What's fun?'

'He's never heard of fun!' Peter whispered. 'I wish we'd never come with him.'

'Stop dawdling!' the Good Guy Guide snapped. 'Come on! Come on!'

Miss Wordsworth searched the playground and the cloakrooms for Ellie and Tom. They were nowhere to be found. Sick with worry, she went back to the classroom to tell Simon and found him flicking through one level after another of the game.

'Any luck?' he asked. She shook her head.

'I've been scanning the game for them. I've been right back to the Crystal Caverns, but there's no sign of them there.' He sat with his head in his hands. 'I'm at a loss. What can we do?'

'We could ask Help I suppose.'

'There isn't one. I haven't linked it up yet.'

'Of course there is, Simon. You don't know your own game!' She sat next to him. 'Look, I'll do it shall I? I've talked to Help quite a lot.'

Simon frowned. He had no idea what she was talking about.

Miss Wordsworth gave him a smile of reassurance and clicked on the Help icon. 'There!'

A smiling Victor Virus appeared, glowing with pleasure. 'Can I help you?'

Simon stared at the face that had haunted his dreams every night for weeks. 'I don't believe it. That's Victor Virus.'

'It's Help. I've been using him all day. Yes, you can help us. Where are Ellie and Tom?'

'More little humans for me?' Victor's smile broadened. He rubbed his hands and his pen flashed. 'You are kind, Miss Wordsworth.'

Simon shook his head in disbelief. 'How did he get in there? I binned him a week ago. He's the program that I created to destroy viruses, but he kept going wrong. I had to write him out.' He shuddered. 'I even had nightmares about him.'

Victor Virus laughed gently. 'Nightmares, Simon? You'll have many more. You can't get rid of me. Miss Wordsworth has been kind enough to give me the power to carry on.'

Miss Wordsworth groaned. She tried to click off the Help icon but Simon motioned to her to leave it.

'What do you want, Victor Virus?' Simon asked.

Victor Virus sneered as if his question were incredibly stupid. 'What do I want, my dear creator? I want to rule Cyberspace. And I will. After all, I have hostages.'

'Poor Josie and Peter!' murmured Miss Wordsworth. 'Those poor children.'

Victor Virus cocked his head to one side. 'Indeed. Josie and Peter. They are doing very well. And Ellie and Tom, did you say? How careless of you to let them play too. But I will make them very welcome in my world.'

'Send them back!' Miss Wordsworth shouted uselessly. Victor Virus laughed.

'Of course, of course. I quite understand your concern. If you want the children back, all you have to do is to link me to the Internet. It's as simple as that.

Perhaps you need a little time to think about it. But a word of warning – Cyber winter is on its way. Your precious children will soon freeze. Goodbye for now.'

'This is worse than my worst nightmare. I've created a monster.'

'We must do what he asks, Simon,' Miss Wordsworth said. 'All we want is to have the children back. It's the only thing that matters.'

Simon shook his head. 'It's not as simple as that. Just think what he's asking us to do! If we link him to the Internet, he'll have control of everything. He'll take over schools, hospitals, governments. There's no knowing where his power might take him. The whole world will be affected.'

The air in the little computer area of the classroom was as cold as ice.

'Then what can we do?' Miss Wordsworth said at last.

'There's only one thing we can do. Sabotage the game. Destroy the whole thing.'

'Simon. The children are in it!'

They looked at each other, the full horror of the situation dawning on their faces. There was absolutely nothing they could do. Victor Virus had them completely in his power.

You're in my power now

'**M**iss Wordsworth. Can we see them now?'
Miss Wordsworth glanced up to see Matthew
and Wendy peering round the side of the bookcase.
'Dinner time's over, Miss Wordsworth.'

Francis pushed past them and ran to the computer.

'Don't touch it Francis,' Simon warned.

'I just want to look at that message again.' Francis
scrolled back. 'There it is. I've got an idea about it.' He
scribbled the words down on a piece of paper. His
tongue was sticking between his teeth with
concentration. AABBQ JT OPU UIF WJSVT. EP OPU ABQ
AABBQ. 'I reckon if we can work out what 'ABQ' stands
for, we've cracked the code. Hey – and there's Josie and
Peter!'

'Oh! Yes! Don't they look lovely!' Annie cried.

The children clustered around, their eyes round with
wonder, huge smiles on their faces.

'They're in some sort of wilderness,' Matthew said.

Francis looked up from his calculations. 'I never got
this far. I didn't even know it existed.'

'That's because I didn't program this level.'

Francis frowned. 'What do you mean?'

Simon leaned forward. He didn't want the other

children to hear this at the moment. 'Remember the black knight that you kept seeing in the first level?'

Francis nodded.

'Well, I know now that it was Victor Virus.'

'The one you binned?'

'He's turned into a virus. He's created this level. My guess is that he's the character with Josie and Peter now. He's in charge. Not me. It's his game now.'

Francis stared at Simon. He had never seen anyone so worried and upset. Then he looked back at the computer screen and the little figures of Josie and Peter trailing behind the guide in black. They looked as worried as Simon.

Peter tripped and grazed his hands on the rough shingle of the track. 'I wish he'd stop.'

'We've been walking and walking for hours,' said Josie. 'We're not getting anywhere, and it all looks the same. And there's no puzzles to solve. How can we ever get out of here?'

The Good Guy Guide turned round and snarled, revealing who he really was – Victor Virus. His flashing smile had gone. His twinkling eyes were hard and steely.

'There is no way out! This is No Hope Valley. My creation. No, there'll be no more puzzles my dears. No little games. No fun.'

Josie felt like crying. She was frightened and angry, and she knew for sure that he had tricked them. 'You lied to us. You said Miss Wordsworth sent you.'

'So she did. I'm very friendly with your Miss Wordsworth. I've just been speaking to her in fact. I've asked her to link me to the Internet in exchange for your freedom.'

Josie sighed with relief. 'Oh, she'll do it, I know she will.'

Victor Virus nodded. 'I'm sure she will. But you needn't think I'll keep my side of the bargain. You're clever little humans, you and the boy. Once I'm out on the Internet I can use your intelligence to guide me through all the other games. That's the first step to conquering Cyberspace.' His eyes gleamed yellow.

'We won't do it,' Peter told him. 'Will we Josie?'

Victor Virus laughed. 'I'm afraid you have no choice, young human. You're in my power now. So you'd better get used to it.'

'I knew he was a fraud,' Josie sniffed.

'No, you didn't. You were the one who followed him first. I wanted to stay with Zzaap.'

Victor Virus swung round again. 'You can forget about that interfering insect once and for all. Now, if you'll excuse me, I have to go and receive your little friends. Miss Wordsworth has sent them in to keep you company. Ellie and Tom. Remember them?'

He laughed, and then thrust his ugly face down towards them.

'So you can stop whining and just wait for me here. Right!'

Richard and Matthew were jostling each other to get the best view of the screen. 'Look at Peter! He's so tiny!' Richard laughed. 'He'd be no use in goal now!'

Oliver was worried. 'Will they have to stay in there forever?'

'How did they get in there?' Wendy asked.

Then Miss Wordsworth did a very brave thing for a teacher. She owned up in front of the whole class. 'It was me. I set a program called "Victor Virus" going, and somehow he sucked them into the game.'

'It was an accident,' Simon said. 'If anyone's to blame it's me – for inventing Victor Virus in the first place.'

'And it isn't just Josie and Peter. I think you all ought to know now that Ellie and Tom are missing as well.'

There was a stunned silence. Oliver burst into tears. 'Not Ellie! What will I tell Mum?'

Miss Wordsworth put a comforting arm round him.

Francis looked up from his scribbling. 'Ellie and Tom!' He jumped up. 'I forgot! I shut them in the music room so they wouldn't play the game. I forgot all about them.'

Miss Wordsworth stood up to follow him. 'Francis Walton –' she began.

He paused, worried. 'Yes, Miss Wordsworth?'

'Well done!'

As she ran down the corridor, Miss Wordsworth could hear loud bangs of drums and the rattle of tambourines coming from the music room. She pushed open the door and total silence fell. Ellie and Tom put down their instruments guiltily.

'Sorry about the noise, Miss Wordsworth,' said Ellie.

'We got bored of waiting,' said Tom.

And Miss Wordsworth smiled at them as though it were her birthday and they'd just given her a present.

'My dear children, I've never been more pleased to see you in my life!'

And there was more good news for Miss Wordsworth when they arrived back in the classroom. Francis had cracked the code and interpreted the Green Man's message.

'Just go back one letter,' he was explaining to Simon. 'A equals Z, B equals A, Q equals P. So the whole message, AABBQ JT OPU UIF WJSVT. EP OPU ABQ AABBQ, translates as 'Zzaap is not the virus. Do not zap Zzaap.'

'The little blue bug,' Simon said quietly. 'Must be. And it's too late. I've already zapped him.'

They all looked at the screen. They could see Josie and Peter sitting on the track in the middle of the grey, stony valley. The sky was heavy with snow. They were shivering, and it looked as if Josie was crying.

'The poor children,' Miss Wordsworth said. 'I can't bear this any longer Simon. We must do what Victor Virus asks us, and get them out.'

But Simon wouldn't hear of it. 'It's much too dangerous. He's a monster. If we unleash him onto the Internet – it doesn't bear thinking about.'

'Maybe that blue bug was trying to help them!'
Francis suggested.

'I think you might be right. But he's gone for good,
whatever he was. No, Victor Virus has us all in his
power. And I created him.'

'And I set him loose!' Miss Wordsworth groaned.

Francis shook his head. Sometimes it seemed as if
grown-ups never got anything right.

'You're right, Peter,' Josie sniffed. 'It's my fault that
we're here. I trusted that man, but you didn't. I wish I'd
believed in Zzaap. And we just left him behind to die.'

'No we didn't.' Peter slipped his rucksack off his back.
'I've got him in here. I couldn't leave him like that.' He
opened up the bag and put the lifeless little body on the
ground.

Caught in a snowstorm

'There he is!' There was an excited shout from Francis and the other children. 'It's Zzaap!'

It was as if the sun had burst through rain clouds. All of a sudden everyone was smiling and shouting.

Simon scrambled past them back to the computer. 'Brilliant! He's not been deleted. We've got another chance. And this time we won't throw it away.'

'Can you program him to be better?' Francis asked. 'Can I help?' His fingers were itching to tap out messages into the computer like Simon.

'You can try,' Simon said. 'Keep feeding me words and I'll translate them into computer equations, and we'll hope for the best. We can do this together.'

'All of us,' Miss Wordsworth said. She was smiling too. 'We can all help. What kind of words do you want, Simon?'

'I know,' Francis said. 'Words that will make Zzaap feel better, or stronger.'

'Like – er – health?' Miss Wordsworth suggested.

Simon typed quickly. 'That's it. More.'

'What about strength?' Francis guessed.

'Power?' suggested Ellie.

'Might! Fight!'

Simon could hardly type fast enough now. 'Great words, great words! Keep them coming!'

'Energy!' said Oliver.

'Force!' Matthew was standing on the chair with excitement.

'Vigour!' Miss Wordsworth shouted, as excited as the rest of them now.

And Francis held out his arms in a gesture of pure rapture. 'Look! Look at him! It's working!'

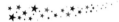

Zzaap rose in the air, his blue wings fluttering. 'Zip zap zee! You don't bury me!'

'Zzaap! You're alive!' Josie shouted. 'We've got you back!'

Peter couldn't speak. His eyes were bright and his throat felt as if he'd just swallowed an egg, whole. He did the only thing that he could have done in the circumstances. He stood on his head and waved his legs in the air.

Turned to ice

In the classroom, all the children were cheering and laughing. Miss Wordsworth quietened them down. There was still a lot of thinking to be done if Josie and Peter were going to be helped. Simon pulled out his grimy handkerchief again.

'Phew! Well done, everybody. I couldn't have done that without your help. Now we've got to get them out of this valley before Victor Virus comes back.'

'Then you can lock him in it and blow him up!' Matthew suggested.

'Precisely,' Simon agreed.

But Francis was still busy thinking. He tapped his pencil against his teeth, the way Simon did sometimes. 'But don't they have to solve puzzles to get out? And there aren't any in this level. He's created a place that doesn't have any. It probably doesn't even have a way out.'

They looked at the screen again. Josie was flapping her arms round, trying to keep warm.

'And it's turning into Cyber winter,' Miss Wordsworth said.

'Leave it to me,' Simon started typing again. 'I'm rolling now. But we'll have to find a way of slowing up Victor Virus or he'll just follow them through.'

'Tie him up with snakes,' Wendy suggested.

'Make the stones slippy so he keeps falling over!' Everybody was coming up with suggestions, but Francis still stayed calm, thinking deeply.

'Miss Wordsworth, you could do it,' he said.

'Me?'

'He talks to you. Pretend you want to help him! You could send him to the wrong place while we get Josie and Peter into the next level.'

She shuddered. 'I feel as if I never want to talk to him again.'

'He's right, Miss Wordsworth. You could trick him,' Matthew urged. 'Send him right back to the Castle of Gloom and lock him in the dungeon!'

'He wouldn't believe they've gone there,' Wendy argued. 'He's clever, not stupid.'

Again, they all started making suggestions. Miss Wordsworth held up her hands.

'OK. Let me hear myself think for a minute.'

They watched her in silence. Ellie was biting her lip. Oliver had his fingers crossed tight. It had to work. It just had to work.

'Welcome back Zzaap,' Josie laughed, as he zipped round her head and between Peter's waving feet.

'Now to get you out of here,' Zzaap said. 'If you can get out of this level, you're nearly at the end of the game. Just don't ask me to meet the Word Master.'

Peter landed back on his feet. His face was bright red from standing upside down for so long. 'I'd forgotten all about the Word Master.'

'We'll worry about him when the time comes,' said Josie, who would rather put him out of her mind completely. 'Just keep moving. It's much too cold to hang around anyway. I just can't see a way out of here at all.'

They set off at a quick pace, not trudging any more, searching round for anything that might show them the way out. The trouble was, everything looked the same. It was as if that stony track wound round the valley and came back to the same place all the time. Then Josie realised that something had changed.

'Look, right up there on the top of the hill. Can you see it? A cairn! That wasn't there before, I'm sure!'

'What's a cairn?' Peter asked.

'It's just a pile of stones. But it shows you where the path goes.'

'Zip zap zee! Well done, Josie!' Zzaap zoomed straight up the mountainside in the direction of the cairn. Josie and Peter tried to follow, but it was much too steep for them.

'We have to zigzag, then it isn't such hard going,' Josie said.

And so they made their way slowly, struggling against the wind, their feet slipping with every step they took. And when they were about halfway up the slope, it began to snow.

'Look at the snow, look at the snow!' Peter shouted. He held out his hands to catch the snowflakes.

Zzaap danced in mid-air with excitement. 'Zip zap zee, so this is what snow is! Hey, it actually makes this dismal old place look pretty! Flakes of snow – what do you know!'

'They look like little apostrophes. Apostrophe snowflakes!' Josie laughed. 'And they aren't melting! Magic!' She scooped up a handful of apostrophes, commas and full stops.

'I'll put some in my bag,' Peter said. 'They might come in useful.'

'You haven't still got any of that cherry pie in there, have you? I could just do with some.'

Peter shook his head. 'I've got all sorts of other things though – like these.' He produced one of the letter fish from the Green Glen.

'What have you got that for?'

'You never know,' he began, and Josie finished it for him, 'it might come in useful!'

The sound of their laughter rang round the valley. Deep in another level, Victor Virus heard it and snarled. Laughter! Was it possible that the little humans were enjoying themselves! He would have to make his way back to No Hope Valley and find out what they were up to.

Zzaap was singing. 'I've never seen snow before. I've always wanted to see snow! Zippy zappy zeedle! They're just like flowers, like little stars, sprinkling down from the sky – what?'

He suddenly realised that Josie was standing with her arms on her hips, calling his name loudly. 'ZZAAP! Are you listening! We have to go on! We won't get anywhere if you turn into a snow-Zzaap. Come on!'

The snow thickened intensely, flurrying and swirling like large white moths, clinging to their hair and eyelashes and sending them into shrieks of laughter. Then it cleared, as if by magic the sky became brilliant blue, and the glittering carpet of snow gleamed like diamonds. And there was a woman dressed in ice-blue, with a crown and necklace made of icicles, and crystals

119

in her hair. She was the most beautiful woman they had ever seen.

'What is the reason for this noise and laughter?' she demanded.

'We're happy because we're leaving No Hope Valley,' Peter said.

The beautiful woman sighed deeply. 'Leaving? Why do you want to leave? Don't you think it's beautiful?'

'Yes, it is now,' Josie said. 'But we have to get out, you see.'

The woman swirled her robes. The hem made sharp crackling sounds on the snow, and blue sparks shot up from them like electricity. 'No, I can't let you go. How could you leave my beautiful snow world?'

'We have to,' Peter tried to explain. He couldn't think why they wanted to go. It was so lovely here now, and she was so sparkly and pretty that he felt he just wanted to gaze at her. 'We have to go home!' he remembered. Home, he frowned. Where was home?

The beautiful woman smiled at him. 'But this is your home. This is your home for ever! I've never met humans before. You will be my little ice humans. Peter,' she kissed him, and her lips left a blue print on his cheeks, 'and Josie. Mine for ever.' She smiled again, and her eyes grew dark and mysterious. 'Remember me?'

Peter felt as though he had been stabbed with ice. He had never felt so cold. 'Oh, I'm freezing! Oh, my heart! She's turning my heart to ice!'

'Remember me! Remember me!' The beautiful woman

swirled round him, and her deep laughter was like an embrace. He flinched away from her, shivering with cold.

'Here Peter, have this,' Josie peeled off her school sweatshirt and slipped it round his shoulders. She rubbed his hands to try to keep him warm. They were blue with cold.

Zzaap buzzed anxiously round them. 'That won't do. It's not enough. Think in your memory. Who is she?'

'Of course! It's a puzzle. We must be back in the word game.'

The woman's eyes glittered. 'Remember me!' she breathed. 'Remember my name! Remember the boy whose heart was turned to ice.'

'Oh, and the girl followed him into the ice palace to save him. And there was a reindeer called Baa-Baa who could talk!'

'Please hurry!' Peter's hair was spiked with icicles. His teeth chattered together. 'I'm so cold!'

'The first word of my name is all around you. The second word means that I rule this world.'

Josie clapped her hands. 'Snow Queen! You're the Snow Queen! And the boy is Kay, and the girl who follows him is Gerda!'

The Snow Queen laughed. 'You have saved your friend!'

The icicles tinkled away from Peter, the colour came back to his cheeks. He took off Josie's sweatshirt and handed it back to her. 'Gosh Josie – thank you! Hey, you saved my life!'

'Just like the girl in the story!' Josie marvelled. 'It's my favourite story now.'

'Zipadoodle! I'd like to read that story sometime!' Zzaap hummed. Then he swung himself upside down. 'But I can't read.'

'I'll teach you,' Josie promised, and Zzaap swung himself the right way up again and landed on her shoulder.

'Will you really! Zip zap zee!'

Peter fished in his bag and brought out his spelling book. 'Here, you can have this if you like.'

'You might as well,' Josie giggled. 'Peter doesn't use it much.'

Zzaap took it from him and opened it up, nearly speechless for once with awe. 'A present from the outside world!' he sighed. 'Never in my wildest dreams did I think this could happen to me.'

Peter turned it the right way up for him. 'It's a bit easier this way.'

'We'd better get going,' Josie said. 'Before that man comes looking for us. How do we get out, Snow Queen Your Majesty?'

'Ask the Stone Man. But how I wish you would stay with me!' Her voice floated away, and she disappeared in a spindrift flurry of snowflakes.

Where are my humans?

Victor Virus was furious. He had searched for Ellie and Tom and realised at last that they were not in the game, and when he returned to the stony track in No Hope Valley where he had left Josie and Peter, that was deserted too. There was some trickery going on, he was sure of that. He had no time to wait for the outside humans to call him up again. He summoned up all his strength and transformed himself into the Help icon, knowing it was his only chance. If Miss Wordsworth communicated with him again, he would collect all the yellow power he needed to carry on.

'Where are my humans?' he roared. His face filled the screen.

The children backed away from the computer, startled by the nastiness in his face and his voice.

'Miss Wordsworth,' Francis urged. 'This is it! Now's your chance! Speak to him!'

Miss Wordsworth rubbed her hands across her face, thinking. Then she sat down in front of the computer. Everyone was watching her. She cleared her throat nervously. 'Erm – hello Victor.'

Victor's face relaxed.

'I'm so sorry,' she went on. 'There's been a bit of a mix-up. It was a mistake you see. Ellie and Tom are still here. I'm very sorry about that.'

Tom and Ellie exchanged worried looks. Was she going to send them in? They weren't sure they wanted to go after all, now that they'd seen Victor Virus. Simon gave them a reassuring wink.

'I see,' said Victor Virus. 'Well, I'm prepared to forgive you if you agree to that other matter.'

Miss Wordsworth crossed her fingers. She smiled nervously. 'Of course. That's not a problem. In fact, we're just about ready to put you on the Internet.'

The children gasped. What on earth was she saying? 'But Miss Wordsworth!' Annie began. Simon put a warning finger to his lips.

Victor Virus almost smiled. He began to look quite handsome again. 'How sensible you are! Now, if you will just tell me where the little humans are . . .'

'Of course. They were last seen going up the snow slopes immediately behind you.'

'The snow slopes! Excellent. Thank you so much for your co-operation.' As they watched, he began to dissolve out of his Help icon shape.

'Will you release the children now?' Miss Wordsworth called.

'Of course, of course,' promised sly Victor Virus.

Miss Wordsworth sank back into her chair. 'Phew!' Simon handed her his handkerchief and she mopped her face with it.

He put his thumbs up. 'Well done! He fell for every word of it!'

'And don't let me catch any of you telling whoppers like that!' Miss Wordsworth warned.

'But why did you send him up the snow slopes?' Oliver asked. 'He's going to find them now.'

'No, he won't. He'll meet the Snow Queen first and she'll turn him into ice,' Francis said.

'Right! And he won't be able to guess her name will he? He doesn't know stories like that!'

'Clever Miss Wordsworth!' The children were jubilant. They turned back to the screen, and now they could see Josie and Peter panting up to the top of the slope, with Zzaap flying a zigzag course between them.

The Stone Man

'What did she mean – ask the Stone Man?' Josie wondered.

Peter stopped and looked back. 'Oh no! He's coming after us!' he groaned.

Far below them they could see the tall figure of Victor Virus, head down against the snow, climbing slowly up the slopes. But even as they were watching, a spiralling whirlwind of snow enveloped him, and there was the Snow Queen, bewitching him with her spell of ice. As she moved away, they could see that he was locked like a statue to the frozen ground.

'Ah! Brilliant!' breathed Peter. 'I'm glad it's happening to him too.'

'That should be the last of him,' Josie said. 'And I've just realised who the Stone Man is. It's the cairn.'

It was indeed the cairn. The nearer they got to him, the less like a random pile of stones he seemed. They were heaped together in the shape of a man, and the top stone was round like a head, and smiling cheerfully at them.

'Welcome, Josie and Peter,' the Stone Man said in a strange, echoey, far-away voice that seemed to be coming from the deep earth beneath him.

'Stone Man, Stone Man,' Josie panted, out of breath after such a steep climb. 'Will you tell us the way out of No Hope Valley?'

'Lift off my head,' the Stone Man said.

'Are you sure?'

The Stone Man smiled. 'Go ahead,' he chuckled. 'Pardon the pun.'

Peter and Josie carefully lifted off his head. He was still chuckling at the time. Underneath it they found a note. Peter frowned at it. 'But it doesn't mean anything. After all that. It's rubbish.'

Josie took it and knelt on the ground, spreading out the paper so they could read it properly: ILL CRUMBLE STONES TO SAND WATER DROWNS LAND MUDS FULL OF PRINTS FOLLOW MY HINTS BEWARE THE MONSTERS IN HIS LAIR.

On the snow slopes below them, the yellow power pen of Victor Virus began to melt his coat of ice. Snow dripped down his body like wax down a candle.

The children in the classroom shrieked a warning and, as if he had heard them, Peter looked up from the strange message. 'I don't believe it, he's thawed the ice!'

Zzaap buzzed round them anxiously. 'It's his yellow power that's doing it. One of your silly humans keeps renewing it. Solve the puzzle and get us out of here.'

'I can't,' Josie said.

'Use the useful things,' Zzaap suggested.

'Useful things? Do you mean the things in my bag?' Peter asked. He opened up his bag. 'Do you mean the snowflakes?'

'Yes!' Josie jumped up excitedly. 'The apostrophe snowflakes. That's exactly what we want. Shake them out.'

Peter shook his bag and out fluttered the apostrophe snowflakes, and some commas and full stops.

'Now we can make sense of it,' Josie said. 'ILL needs an apostrophe and it turns into 'I'll . . .'

'I'll crumble stones to sand – full stop,' suggested Peter. 'Hey, look at that! The Stone Man's falling to bits!'

It was true. The cairn was collapsing into grains of sand.

'It must be meant to happen. Carry on,' Josie said. 'I need another full stop. Now it reads: I'll crumble stones to sand. Water drowns land, full stop. Now look!'

The grains of sand had soaked up the water on the ground and had turned into mud.

Josie placed another apostrophe and a full stop. 'Mud's full of prints. So it is! Wow!' Footprints appeared in the mud.

But Peter had seen Victor Virus. 'He's coming. Try a full stop after hints. Follow my hints.'

'Quick. I've got it. Another comma. And an apostrophe.' Josie stuck them into place. 'Beware, the monster's in his lair . . .'

'FULL STOP!' shouted Zzaap. The muddy footprints started running. 'Follow them!'

'I'm not sure I want to,' said Josie.

'Go on! Go on!' shouted Simon. He was standing on his chair waving his arms about. 'It's the right way!'

Victor Virus's laughter chimed round the slopes. 'I've got you now! You'll never get away from me.' He was nearly at the top, striding fast.

'It's either the monster or him,' Peter said. 'We can do it, Josie. Let's go for it.' He stepped into the muddy footprints and started to run with them towards a buttress of rock. Reluctantly, Josie followed him. An oily mist swirled around them, and they could see nothing behind them or in front of them, only the footprints that soundlessly trod the ground. A cleft appeared in the rock, swinging slowly open like a door. The muddy footprints slopped into it, and together they followed.

But Zzaap didn't. As soon as they were at a safe distance, he turned back to face Victor Virus. Very soon, Josie and Peter would reach the final level, and they would be face to face with the Word Master and at his mercy. Zzaap had no wish to follow them there. But he wasn't going to let Victor Virus follow them there either. He and Victor were alone at last in No Hope Valley, and each stood still, staring at the other. This was the moment they had both been waiting for.

Victor Virus raised his power pen. Zzaap powered his light. They both fired. For a second all the rocks and the stones and the sky flashed with brilliant blue and yellow lights. Peter and Josie paused outside the dark mouth of a cave. The muddy footsteps disappeared into it.

'Come on,' Peter said. 'We have to leave them to it now.'

And they plunged into the cave, and the fissure in the rock closed up behind them.

Level five

WRD MSTR

The monster's lair

'Where have they gone?' Ellie asked. 'I can't see them any more.'

'I think I know,' said Francis. 'It's the worst bit, isn't it, Simon?'

'It's pretty scary, even from the outside,' Simon admitted. 'But what it's going to be like for them, actually being there, I just don't like to think. It must be absolutely terrifying.'

It was. At first there was nothing to see. The cave was pitch black, and there was a sound of something huge, breathing heavily as if it were in a deep sleep.

'Where are we?' Josie whispered, and just as she said it, the sleeping thing woke up and let out a bellowing roar. Flames gushed from its mouth and acrid yellow smoke billowed from its nostrils. An enormous black shadow loomed up and lumbered towards them.

'Oh no!' Francis breathed. 'They've woken the monster up.'

'What can they do?' Wendy asked. 'It's horrible! Look at its eyes.'

'They have to guess his name, don't they?' Matthew said. 'Or he'll eat them alive.'

The voice of the monster hissed around them, licking them with the tips of flames. Pungent yellow smoke that was as rank as seaweed billowed with every word.

'*Out of the mist-swirls you enter my lair*
Fire-flames flicker
Stinging smoke smarts.
Look into your mind-holes
Know my name
Or the hooks of my talons will tear your hearts.'

The children in the classroom were white with tension. They could hear every word now, every swish of the monster's tail, the scrape of his claws on the floor of the cave. Wendy was sobbing quietly into the hem of her skirt. Miss Wordsworth put her arm round her.

'I think I know who it is,' Ellie breathed.

'So do I,' whispered Francis. His fists were clenched so tight on the desk that his knuckles looked like white marbles. 'Come on, Peter. You know it! You love this story!'

'Shh!' said Tom. 'I can't hear what they're saying.'

Peter banged his fists together. 'You're Grendel!' he shouted. 'Now go away!'

Grendel sucked in his flames. He twisted round them, his long tail thrashing from side to side, his nostrils flaring, his eyes blazing like yellow lamps. He hissed again.

'Out of the hall of Heorot came
One who destroyed me in the ocean's deep
Never give utterance to his name
Or I will slide into everlasting sleep.'

Peter closed his eyes. 'What does he mean? I don't know what he means.'

'Don't panic,' Josie whispered. 'Everlasting sleep means death. If we say someone's name, Grendel will die. But whose name?'

Miss Wordsworth was murmuring softly to herself, her eyes shut tight as if she was chanting in her sleep. 'Out of the halls of Heorot came, one who destroyed me in the ocean's deep . . .'

Francis thumped the desk. 'Say it Peter. Say it! Who killed Grendel?'

And Peter shouted at the top of his voice, 'Beowulf!'

With a hiss like the sound of water quenching flames, the monster Grendel slumped to the floor and lay as still as stone. Peter and Josie stepped over his prone body and walked through the corridor of smoke.

'Ah, Peter, you're a genius!' Francis shouted. Miss Wordsworth opened her eyes.

'I knew it too,' Matthew boasted.

'Yes, but you weren't about to be eaten alive by Grendel were you?' said Ellie scornfully. 'It makes a big difference, you know.'

A bell rang in the corridor. 'I'd completely forgotten what time it is,' Miss Wordsworth said. 'Simon, it's the end of afternoon break. Forty minutes from now, Peter and Josie's mothers will be here to collect them. What are we going to do?'

Simon shook his head. He was still dazed from that encounter with Grendel. He felt as if he'd been in the lair with them. 'We can't do anything. We'll have to tell them the truth.'

'Of course we will. And they'll tell the police, naturally. I'll lose my job. You and your game will be taken into custody. And Josie and Peter will still be running round inside it.'

'I wonder what happened to Zzaap?' Francis asked. 'Did he win, or did Victor Virus, or what?'

'There's only one way to find out.' Miss Wordsworth clicked on the Help icon. 'I'm afraid if Victor Virus is still here, we'll know that he's destroyed Zzaap.'

'I don't want to know,' said Wendy. But it was too late. Victor Virus had come up on screen. He was enveloped in the yellow smoke of Grendel's lair, and he was choking.

'Looks as if you need help now,' Miss Wordsworth said.

Victor Virus nodded, clutching his throat and gasping for air. 'Get me out of here.'

'Don't!' Tom and Matthew begged.

'I want you to release our children. Now!' Miss Wordsworth demanded.

Victor Virus spluttered. 'My dear Miss Wordsworth. I cannot release them if I am not with them. Release me from this monster and I promise I will let them go. Your little humans will be free. You have my word.' He coughed violently. 'Please, I beg you, get me out of here.' And he sank back into the greeny-yellow swirl of Grendel's smoke.

'Over to you,' Miss Wordsworth said to Simon. 'Programme the answers to him.'

'We can't do it. We can't trust him. He's more of a monster than Grendel is.'

'Simon, it's our only chance. Zzaap has lost! Those children have no one to help them. Surely the only thing that matters now is to get them out by half-past three. And look at the time now.'

'Yes, get them out,' begged Ellie. 'I want Josie back.'

The children turned to each other, arguing fiercely. Half of them agreed with Miss Wordsworth and Ellie, the other half with Simon.

'You can't believe a word Victor Virus says,' Matthew insisted. 'What if we let him on to the Internet and he still doesn't free them?'

'He might leave them in the game. They'd stay there for ever,' said Tom. 'What do you think, Francis?'

They turned to him eagerly. He wasn't like Simon or Miss Wordsworth. He didn't have to worry about what parents thought or what the police did. He would know the best thing to do, surely.

'We mustn't let Victor Virus out,' he said. There was a cheer of support and agreement. 'At least while he's in Grendel's lair we've got him trapped.'

Little Ellie jumped up excitedly. 'Zap him while he's in there!'

But yet again Simon shook his head. 'I can't zap

him. I've tried. Somehow he keeps getting more power from somewhere. If he's going to be zapped at all, it's got to be by someone inside the game.'

Francis was scanning rapidly, hopelessly. 'But not by Zzaap. I can't see him at all. I can't even get into No Hope Valley. It must be closed off.'

They all slumped back into their chairs or onto the floor. There was nothing they could do but watch and hope.

'It's five past three,' Miss Wordsworth murmured. 'And we don't even know where Josie and Peter are now.'

Simon took over the joystick. 'I know where they should be,' he said. 'They should just about have reached the Word Hoard Treasury. And if they get through there –' he sighed deeply. 'Heaven help them. They'll meet the Word Master himself.'

The Word Hoard Treasury

Peter and Josie pushed open the door at the end of
the smoky tunnel and found themselves in a room
that was piled high with boxes of words, words on
hooks, words on hangers, shelves of words and words
dripping out of half-open drawers. A scarecrow was
picking through them, humming cheerfully to himself.

'Ah, there you are Josie and Peter! A bit of help at
last. The Master told me there might be some little
humans along one day to give me a hand. I'd almost
given up on you. I'm pleased to meet you though, very

pleased. You might as well get to work straight away.'

Josie smiled at him. How peaceful it was in here! 'What would you like us to do?'

The scarecrow scratched his head. Bits of straw drifted down to the floor and Josie picked them up and handed them to him. He stuffed them back under his battered old hat. 'Well, you see, this is the Master's word hoard, and I'm sorting them out for him.'

'They have to be in alphabetical order,' Josie suggested, gazing round at the mess, 'or you'll never sort them out.'

The scarecrow smiled. 'I wish I'd thought of that! But first, we have to mend all the broken ones.'

'How did they get broken?'

'You've no idea how badly some people treat words. They just throw them about as if they weren't worth anything. I was a broken word once. Half of me was in that box there, and the other half was at the bottom of that cupboard. *Scare* and *crow*. Anyway, I'm all right now, and that's the main thing.' He started whistling again, and rummaged through a box. He brought out the word *star* and held it up. 'Now, where's the other half of this gone?'

'Will this do?' Josie found *light* sticking out of another box and held it up – *starlight*.

Scarecrow put his hands on his hips. 'Looks perfect to me. Stick them together and hang it up to dry, there's a good little human. Next to *rainbow* there. Lovely word, rainbow. Fancy anyone breaking it. Vandals!'

Josie hung *starlight* up between a perfect rainbow and a cascading waterfall. Her word unfolded like a curtain and turned dark blue, shimmering with the diamond lights of thousands of stars.

'Oh my! Isn't that pretty!' Scarecrow stood back to admire it. 'Starlight! That's going to be one of my favourite words, that is.'

'Can we go now?' Peter asked.

'Oh, do you really want to?' Scarecrow frowned. 'What a shame! But I'm sorry to tell you that the way out word has been broken too. Never mind, we'll find the bits somewhere.' He gazed round at the mess of words. 'What have you got there, girl human?'

Josie held up the word *wood*.

'I know there's another bit to that somewhere. Try that brown box.'

Josie knelt down and rummaged into the box. '*Snow, song, night, bell – land*,' she shouted. 'I've found it!'

'Definitely!' Scarecrow was as excited as she was. 'Here's the glue. Stick 'em together and hang it up to dry. Ah! Just look at that! Nothing sweeter than a patch of woodland, I always say.'

As the curtain draped open, sunlight came in dapples through leafy green, and the room was filled with the sound of birdsong.

'What do you think, Peter?' Josie turned to him, her eyes shining. But Peter was busy groping round the walls trying to find an opening in them. Josie turned back to the boxes.

'I've found *man*,' Josie said. 'Shall I stick him to *snow*?'

'Mansnow,' Scarecrow muttered. 'No such word.'

'Snowman. I'll show you.' She stuck the words together and hung them on a coat hanger, and a sparkling snowman beamed down at them, huffing frosty breath from his mouth.

'Fancy that!' Scarecrow marvelled. 'Well, you meet a new word every day. I'd never have thought of that one. Here you are – *butter*. Quite a few words go with that one. Any one will do. You choose.'

'Josie!' Pete turned round impatiently. 'We can't stay here.'

But Josie was having a wonderful time. 'I've got *cup* here. And *fly*. Which one shall I have, Scarecrow?'

'Hmm. They're both nice, very nice. It's hard to choose. Tell you what. Let's have *cup*. Nice bit of yellow.'

Josie hung up a golden field of buttercups. 'I'll hang on to *fly* though. I might come across *dragon* somewhere.'

Scarecrow clapped his twiggy hands together. 'Ooh, you are enjoying yourself! I knew you would. Made for this job you are.'

Peter stood between them. 'Josie, we're trying to get out of here!' he reminded her. In the classroom Miss Wordsworth muttered, 'Exactly! Hurry up, for goodness sake! It's ten past three!'

Scarecrow sighed. 'Well, I don't want you to go. It's so nice to have a bit of company. But you're quite right.

There is a way out.' He pulled the word *door* out of a pocket in his raggedy trousers. 'You'll have to find the other half.'

Peter grabbed it and hunted through a box. '*Fire*,' he said. '*Work . . .*'

'That's a word!' Josie said.

'Leave it,' Peter warned. '*Box. Wind. Sun. Way*. Way!' he jumped up and clamped the two halves together. 'Got it! *Doorway*!'

He hung the word up, and down billowed the curtain with the sound of a great, rushing wind, framing the doorway with brightly-coloured banners. And inside the doorway stood a towering figure in a cloak that sizzled and flashed with lightning. It was the Word Master himself.

The Word Master himself

There was a gasp of awe from the children in the classroom. Ellie hid her face in her hands.

'I want Mum!' Oliver gasped. Ellie held his hand tightly.

Francis stared, wide-eyed and shaking. 'So that's the Word Master. Wow!'

'He's really something,' Simon agreed, marvelling at his own creation. 'And to think I programmed him.'

The Word Master stepped back and, as if they were hypnotised, Josie and Peter followed him into his room. Hundreds and thousands of books lined the shelves on the walls; every book that had ever been written in the world, parchment scrolls and carved tablets, leather books with gold lettering, shiny picture books. Some people were sitting at high wooden desks, scribbling and thinking and muttering quietly to themselves.

The Word Master clapped his hands and a shower of letters, as bright as fireworks, shimmered round him. He juggled them into words, and every time he moved, different letters spangled round him, new words, changing and reforming. They reminded Peter of the

flocks of starlings he saw over the valley at home,
drifting and surging and winding into different shapes.
Home! Where was that?

'No need to ask you my name,' said the Word
Master. His voice was quiet and firm. 'I am the Master
of Wordworld. You've come to the end of your trail.
You've come to your final trial.'

Peter gulped. He had never been more frightened in his life, but it was difficult to know why. The Word Master was the most wonderful person he had ever seen, and yet there was something about him that was utterly terrifying. He and Josie edged closer together.

'We'll be all right, Peter,' she whispered.

'Right?' the Word Master repeated. 'Write that down!' He flourished a stick of magic chalk out of the air, and handed it to her.

Her hands were shaking. Nervously, she wrote the word in the air with it, as if she was writing with chalk on a board, and there the letters hung and sparkled. *RIGHT*.

The Word Master swung round to look at Peter. 'Can you do spells?'

'No, sir,' Peter whispered. He cleared his throat and said it again.

'What is the rule of the I and the E, especially when they come after C?'

Peter gaped. His mind was a complete blank.

'Take it. Take it,' the Word Master said sternly. Then his eyes seemed to flicker with a kind of sunlight, and his voice softened. 'I give. You take. You –?'

'Receive!' The fog in Peter's mind cleared away. 'I before E except after C. That's the rule!'

The Word Master laid one hand on Peter's head, and one on Josie's. 'You are conjurers of words, masters of spells. Sit down for the test.'

Peter and Josie made puzzled faces at each other. The other people at the desks paused for a brief second, and smiled vaguely, as though they were deep in thought, and then carried on writing. Most of them were talking out loud as they wrote.

'Far away from here, at the edge of a forest, there lived a little girl and her mother,' a girl in a red cloak said.

A man in a suit of red and yellow murmured, 'Hamlin town's in Brunswick, by ancient Hanover city . . .'

And a boy in ragged clothes said triumphantly, 'He held up his bowl, and begged for more!'

'Fee fie foe fum!' rumbled a giant who was much too big for his desk.

'I know who they are!' Josie marvelled, 'They're –'

'Shh!' warned the Word Master. 'Don't break their spell. They're busy writing stories about themselves. That's their test. Yours is yet to come. The greatest test of all.'

Josie and Peter looked nervously at each other. Josie bit her lip. Peter closed his eyes. Pens and quills and pencils scribbled rapidly around them.

'Well?' the Word Master demanded. 'What are you waiting for?'

'We're waiting for the questions, sir,' said Josie.

'You must ask the questions.'

'But – if we ask the questions, who's going to answer them?' asked Peter.

The Word Master pointed and the cowering shape of Victor Virus appeared. He was coughing and sneezing, shivering and rubbing his hands together with cold. He saw Josie and Peter and hissed at them.

The Word Master swung Victor Virus round to face him. 'How dare you invade my Wordworld!' he roared.

Victor Virus cowered away from him.

'How dare you bring humans into our space, into our precious Cyberspace?'

'Me, Word Master?'

The Word Master swirled round, causing lightning sparks to shiver angrily round Victor Virus's feet. 'They can never be part of our world. You have broken the rules.'

Victor Virus bowed his head. 'Word Master, forgive me. I'm not well. I've been through water and ice and fire.'

The Word Master laughed. 'And to water and ice and fire you belong until you leave this game.'

'I'll leave now,' Victor Virus began, but the Word Master held up his hand.

'There is only one way out. You have to pass the test.'

He pointed again and a blue-winged bug appeared.

'Zzaap!' Peter shouted with relief. 'You're here too!'

Zzaap blinked and shimmied his wings to see if they still worked. 'So I am!' he buzzed. 'Zip zap zee! I am! I'm here. One minute I'm upside down in a ditch and the next minute I'm – oh!' He saw the Word Master and lowered his voice respectfully. 'I'm in the Word Master's library. Uh-oh.'

'Zzaap,' said the Word Master. His voice was terrifyingly quiet. 'Why have you failed in your mission?'

Zzaap hummed thoughtfully.

'No virus gets to this level, Zzaap. And yet you have let him through! Why does he have so much power? And why haven't you got rid of him before now?'

Zzaap stopped humming. 'Master, I would have destroyed him, but I wanted to help these little humans.' His voice tailed off, as if he had surprised himself by saying it.

'They have no place in this world of ours,' the Word Master reminded him sternly.

'I know,' Zzaap buzzed. 'But they saved my life, Master.'

'Pah! I want you all out of my game, the whole lot of you. None of you belong here. But the only way out is to play the game to the very end. All the players are present. Only one person can win.'

'But Peter and I are together,' Josie began.

'You are not the contestants.' The Word Master snapped his fingers impatiently, causing electric sparks to shiver into the air. They drifted up to the ceiling and hung like bright moths, watching eagerly. 'The contestants are Victor Virus and Zzaap. It is their final battle. Whoever wins will take Josie and Peter out of the game.'

There was a chilled silence that seemed to last for ever. The Word Master climbed up to his chair. It was polished so deeply that everything in the room was reflected in its arms and legs – the books, the scribbling story-writers, Josie and Peter, Zzaap and Victor Virus.

'If the virus wins, you will go into Cyberspace with him.'

'For ever!' Victor Virus promised, a ghost of his old charming smile playing round his lips.

'And if Zzaap wins.'

'Zippydee, I'll take you straight home.'

'Correct.' The Word Master inclined his head. He lifted up an ancient wooden sand-timer and placed it in front of him. He looked at Josie and Peter. 'Ask your questions. And prove that your time has not been wasted while you've been in my game. Your time starts –' he turned over the sand-timer, 'now.'

The great trial

'**W**ow!' breathed Francis. 'That's really scary, that is.'

'Where are they going to get the questions from?' Tom asked.

'And it's not fair – Zzaap can't read or write,' said Matthew.

'Shh! I want to listen.' Ellie squirmed in front of them and lay on her stomach, her chin propped on her hands. Miss Wordsworth looked at the clock. A quarter past three. A desperate silence settled over everyone.

'I can't think of anything to ask,' Peter whispered. 'Can you?'

Josie shook her head. 'Why don't we look at the things we picked up on the way here? You put them in your bag.'

'Good idea. It's a start anyway.' Peter shook his bag and tipped it up. Three pebbles rolled out. Josie grabbed one.

'This'll do.' She held it up. 'Spell this, and give me another word with the same ending.'

Victor Virus smirked. 'P-e-b-b-l-e. And bubble.'

'Two points to Victor Virus,' announced Word Master.

'It's not fair on Zzaap,' Peter whispered.

'I can spell some things,' Zzaap buzzed. 'B-l-u-e. Z-z-a –'

'Oh, Zzaap. Use the book! The spell book!' Josie hissed.

'What? Oh yes!' Zzaap opened Peter's spelling book and looked at it delightedly. 'Peter gave me this! A present from the outside world.'

'Answer the question!' Word Master roared.

'What question?' Zzaap asked, worried.

'I haven't asked it yet,' said Josie

Zzaap held the book up and zipped through the pages at lightning speed. His antennae shivered. Then he shut the book and gabbled at top speed.

'Abcdefghijklmnopqrstuvwxy-zip-zap-zee! I like it!'

Peter groaned. 'Rock. Tell me three meanings of the word rock.'

'Hijkl,' hummed Zzaap.

'It's a stone,' said Victor Virus.

'One point to Victor Virus.'

'Ijkl. Mno,' said Zzaap.

'Answer the question!' everyone in the classroom roared.

Zzaap whizzed round the Word Master's library. 'Pqr –' He stopped on top of a book of nursery rhymes and sang very sweetly, 'Rock-a-bye-baby, on a tree top . . .'

'One point to Zzaap.'

Zzaap fell off the bookcase in excitement and flicked himself over in mid-air. 'Zip zap zee! I got a point! I got a point! Stuv. Wxyzip-zap-zed! Erm . . . r-o-c-k – sweet sticky pink stuff – rots your teeth if you've got any.'

'Correct,' said the Word Master. 'At the end of this round, Zzaap has two points.'

'Yeah!' Zzaap cart-wheeled madly round the desks, knocking the quill out of Little Red Riding Hood's hand. Oliver Twist picked it up and handed it back to her.

'Next question.'

'Come on Zzaap!' Miss Wordsworth shouted.

'What else is in the bag?' Josie asked.

Peter rummaged about and pulled out a half-eaten roasted chestnut. 'Erm – I know. Give me two words beginning with 'c-h'.'

'And two words ending with 'c-h',' Josie added. They both glared at Zzaap, who was eating the spelling book.

'Abc – chirpy, that's me!' he said.

Victor Virus stood up. 'Champion, that's me! Pinch. Punch. It's a cinch.'

'At the end of round three, Victor Virus leads by seven points to three,' said the Word Master. 'And the sand-timer is two-thirds empty.'

Zzaap burped loudly. Letters floated out of his mouth and drifted round the room. 'Pardon me!'

'He's getting good,' laughed Francis.

'Yeah, but he's four points behind,' Matthew pointed out.

'Three twenty-five!' Miss Wordsworth moaned. 'Come on Zzaap!'

Peter delved into his rucksack again and produced a bunch of keys.

'Spell keys,' said Josie. 'And spell another word that sounds the same.'

Miss Wordsworth breathed in sharply. 'Ooh, that's hard, Josie!'

'GhijK,' Zzaap hummed.

With one voice all the children in the classroom shouted, 'K-E-Y-S.'

'Shush!' said Simon. 'You've missed it! Victor Virus has just got another point.'

The children settled down again, hardly daring to breathe.

Zzaap zizzed along the bookshelves again. He stopped by the shipping section.

'Opq,' he said dreamily. 'Q is followed by u – the place you keep boats in – q-u-a – rstuvwx – y! Quays!'

'Brilliant!' shouted Josie, and all the children in the classroom at home with her.

'At the end of this round,' said the Word Master. 'Victor Virus has seven . . . eight points, Zzaap has four.'

'It's not fair!' Francis shouted. 'Zzaap answered a really hard question then. He should have got extra points.'

'Three minutes left,' said Miss Wordsworth.

Peter shook out his bag. Eight fish landed on the desk. 'Erm?'

'OK,' Josie said. 'The letter fish.' She spread them out to spell the words 'GREEN MAN'. 'How many vowels are here, and how many consonants?'

'A-e-i-o-u,' burped Zzaap. 'Two 'ee's, one 'a'. Three vowels, five of the other things.'

'Correct. One point.' The Word Master glanced at the sand-timer.

'And FOR TWO POINTS,' said Peter indignantly, 'take away all the letters that are the same. What word is left?'

'Good boy!' whispered Miss Wordsworth.

'Two 'ee's. Two 'n's. Leaves g-r-a-m. Gram,' Zzaap buzzed.

'Correct.' The Word Master had to raise his voice over Zzaap's ecstatic buzzing. 'At the end of this round, Victor Virus has eight points, Zzaap has seven.'

'COME ON ZZAAP!' The children in the classroom went wild. Oliver lay on his back, kicking his legs in the air.

'All that's left in the bag are three apostrophes,' said Peter.

'OK. Put the three apostrophes into this sentence.' Josie waved her magic chalk and wrote in the air – *Its one o clock and the cats eaten all its sausages*. Then she turned the sentence round so Victor Virus and Zzaap could see it.

'*It* apostrophe *s one o* apostrophe *clock and* –' Zzaap began.

'*The cat* apostrophe *s eaten all its sausages*,' Victor Virus snapped. Oily sweat was dripping down his forehead. He wiped it away with the back of his hand and flipped it over Zzaap.

'Hey, shouldn't there be an apostrophe in *its sausages*?' Zzaap demanded, his hands on his hips.

'No! Lose a point!' shouted the Word Master. 'At the end of this round, Victor Virus has nine, Zzaap has eight.'

Simon pulled out his handkerchief again. 'Less than a minute to go!'

There was a familiar rumble in the road outside the classroom. The school bus had arrived. Three cars pulled up at the gates.

'The parents are here!' moaned Miss Wordsworth. She pulled at the silver chain round her wrist and snapped it in half. She didn't even notice.

'My bag's empty,' said Peter helplessly. 'We haven't got any more questions.'

'I will ask the last question,' the Word Master said. 'The winner will be the one who makes the most words out of my name.'

Tick, tock, went the classroom clock.

Trickle, sheesh, went the sands of time.

'Stream. Dream,' Victor Virus said.

'Same. Roam,' said Zzaap.

'Dame. Made. Mode,' said Victor Virus.

'Dome. Tea. Team. Seam,' said Zzaap.

Tom and Matthew hugged each other. 'Neck and neck!' they yelled. 'Fourteen points each!'

'Road. Draw. Drawer,' said Victor Virus.

'Mast. Waste,' said Zzaap.

'Victor Virus seventeen. Zzaap sixteen,' said the Word Master.

'Toad. Raw,' said Victor Virus.

'Tow. Toe,' said Zzaap.

'Please. Please. Please,' said Francis.

'Victor Virus nineteen, Zzaap eighteen,' said the Word Master.

Total silence. One grain left in the sand-timer.

And Zzaap floated soundlessly out of his chair and said, 'Word! and Master!'

eybdooG paazZ

At that point, the roof nearly lifted off the school. 'He's won! Zzaap's won!' Everyone was delirious with excitement and joy.

Zzaap zizzed round the Word Master's library like a turbo-bug. 'Zip zap zeeeeee!'

Victor Virus crumpled into a heap. The Word Master screwed him into a ball and dropped him into the wastepaper basket, where he disintegrated into a heap of computer hieroglyphs.

'Children, you have done well,' the Word Master said kindly. 'Go through that door, please.'

Josie and Peter were both in a daze.

'After you,' Zzaap buzzed.

They walked through a door marked Word Master's Study and emerged in their own classroom.

They couldn't take anything in at first – Simon collapsed in front of the computer; Matthew and Tom standing on a chair, shouting their heads off; Miss Wordsworth hugging Francis; everyone in the room shouting crazily and dancing and whooping; an abandoned Viking longboat.

'There's Mum,' said Peter.

'There's Dad,' said Josie. They waved to their parents through the window.

Simon came round and mopped his face.

'Simon, your game's brilliant,' Peter said.

Josie agreed. 'I knew it would be! You were really good at it, Peter.'

Peter grinned. 'So were you.'

Ellie and Tom clamoured round Simon. 'Can we play it tomorrow? Please? It's only fair!'

And Francis, recovered from his embarrassing experience, looked round him. 'But where's Zzaap?'

Zzaap was gazing at a message on the computer screen:

Message for super-insect Zzaap. Computer jam in Cyber Park.

Simon rushed to the window, but all he could see was a trail of blue stars shooting off into space, and all he could hear was a voice buzzing far away:

'Zip zap zee! Another job for me!'